PENGUIN  CLASSICS

ICE

ANNA KAVAN (1901–1968) was born Helen Woods. She began her career writing under her married name Helen Ferguson, publishing six novels. It was only after she had a nervous breakdown that she became Anna Kavan, the protagonist of her 1930 novel *Let Me Alone*, with an outwardly different persona and a new literary style. Much of her life remains an enigma, but her talent was nonetheless remarkable, and her works have been compared to those of Doris Lessing, Virginia Woolf, and Franz Kafka. Kavan suffered periodic bouts of mental illness and long-term drug addiction—she became addicted to heroin in the 1920s and continued to use it throughout her life—and these facets of her life feature prominently in her work. Her widely admired works include *Asylum Piece*, *I Am Lazarus*, and *Julia and the Bazooka* (published posthumously). She died in 1968 of heart failure, soon after the publication of her most celebrated work, *Ice*.

JONATHAN LETHEM is the *New York Times* bestselling author of nine novels, including *Dissident Gardens*, *Chronic City*, *The Fortress of Solitude*, and *Motherless Brooklyn*, and of the essay collection *The Ecstasy of Influence*, which was a National Book Critics Circle Award finalist. A recipient of the MacArthur Fellowship and winner of the National Book Critics Circle Award for Fiction, Lethem's work has appeared in *The New Yorker*, *Harper's Magazine*, *Rolling Stone*, *Esquire*, and *The New York Times*, among other publications.

KATE ZAMBRENO is the author of the novels *Green Girl* and *O Fallen Angel*, as well as two works of experimental nonfiction, *Heroines* and *Book of Mutter*. She is at work on a series of books about time, memory, and the persistence of art. She teaches in the writing programs at Sarah Lawrence College and Columbia University.

ANNA KAVAN

Ice

50TH ANNIVERSARY EDITION

Foreword by
JONATHAN LETHEM

Afterword by
KATE ZAMBRENO

PENGUIN BOOKS

PENGUIN BOOKS
An imprint of Penguin Random House LLC
375 Hudson Street
New York, New York 10014
penguin.com

First published in Great Britain by Peter Owen Ltd 1967
First published in the United States of America by Doubleday & Company, Inc. 1970
This edition with a foreword by Jonathan Lethem and an afterword
by Kate Zambreno published in Penguin Books 2017

Published by arrangement with Peter Owen Publishers, London.

The afterword by Kate Zambreno first appeared as "Anna Kavan" in *Context*, issue 18.

LIBRARY OF CONGRESS CATALOGING-IN-PUBLICATION DATA
Names: Kavan, Anna, 1901–1968, author.
Title: Ice / Anna Kavan ; foreword by Jonathan Lethem ; afterword by Kate Zambreno.
Description: 50th anniversary edition. | New York : Penguin Books, 2017.
Identifiers: LCCN 2017018717 (print) | LCCN 2017018810 (ebook) | ISBN
9780525503774 (ebook) | ISBN 9780143131991 (paperback)
Subjects: | BISAC: FICTION / Literary. | GSAFD: Science fiction.
Classification: LCC PR6009.D63 (ebook) | LCC PR6009.D63 I24 2017 (print) |
DDC 823/.912—dc23
LC record available at https://lccn.loc.gov/2017018717

Printed in the United States of America
5   7   9   10   8   6   4

Set in Sabon LT Std

Contents

Foreword

Gazing at Ice

Anna Kavan's *Ice* is a book like the moon is the moon. There's only one. It's cold and white, and it stares back, both defiant and impassive, static and frantically on the move, marked by phases, out of reach. It may even seem to be following you. It is a book that hides, and glints, like "the girl" who is at the center of its stark, fable-like tableau of catastrophe, pursuit, and repetition-compulsion. The tale might seem simple: a desperate love triangle played out in a world jarred into eco-catastrophe by political and scientific crimes. The narrator, whose resolute search for the girl might appear at first benign or even heroic, nonetheless slowly converges with the personality and motives of the sadistic, controlling "warden," who is the book's antagonist and the narrator's double. Though *Ice* is always lucid and direct, nothing in it is simple, and it gathers to itself the properties of both a labyrinth and a mirror.

Like the girl, and like the book's author, *Ice* attracts fascination and would-be sponsors. Published in 1967, the book has been introduced by Brian Aldiss, Christopher Priest, Anaïs Nin (whose introduction for the first edition was rejected by Kavan), and now myself. *Ice* has also generated admiring comments by Doris Lessing and L. P. Hartley, and critical appraisals by L. Timmel Duchamp, Elizabeth Young, and Kate Zambreno—and Kavan has already been the subject of two biographies. Perhaps, given the comparison—and since the brittle, damaged, entrancing "girl" hardly thrives in the enclosures devised for her by the narrator and the warden—you should probably suspect all our motives and go past these words, to the pages of *Ice* itself.

I first located *Ice* in a used bookstore, in its first American edition, published by Doubleday after Kavan's death and introduced by Aldiss, who called it science fiction. This was during the time in my reading life when I was trying so hard to find something more like Philip K. Dick and J. G. Ballard and a handful of other things (including certain of Aldiss's own books, like *Report on Probability A*). But Kavan's *Ice* wasn't more of anything. I doubt it helps for it to be categorized as science fiction, or to be categorized at all. Even given Anna Kavan's remarkable life story, and amid her shelf of coolly anguished fiction, *Ice* stands alone.

Kavan wasn't her real name—or perhaps I should say it wasn't her first name. Born Helen Woods to an upper-class British family, then twice miserably married to older alcoholics, she published several novels under her first married name, Helen Ferguson. From these books, which were precise and despairing, if conventional by the standard of her later writing, she seized up for her self-invention the name of her own autobiographical character: Anna Kavan. The details of her long traipse through wartime exile, multiple suicide attempts, psychiatric incarcerations, and decades of heroin addiction could fill books; Kavan filled sixteen novels with them, though her preference was to sublimate autobiography into pensive, dislocated, and somewhat numbed tableaux.

The frozen disaster overtaking the planet in *Ice* evokes that cold-war, bomb-dreading, postwar twentieth century we still, in many ways, live inside; it echoes images as popular as episodes of Rod Serling's *Twilight Zone* or Kurt

Vonnegut's *Cat's Cradle*. The presentation is scattered with scenes of war, civil unrest, and collective societal dysfunction, both vivid and persuasive. During World War II Kavan journeyed by steamer slowly from New Zealand to various ports, including New York, and at last returning to England. A realistic novelist might have made some epic like Olivia Manning's *Balkan* and *Levant* trilogies from this, but Kavan wasn't a maker of epics and was accompanied not by a colorful husband but by her own violent solitude. A crushed-down and imagistic epic of flight may lurk in the interstices of *Ice*, in fact. Yet as in Kafka, Poe, Kōbō Abe, and Ishiguro's *The Unconsoled*, the essential disturbance resides in an inextricable interplay between inner and outer worlds.

Kavan's commitment to subjectivity was absolute, but in this, her greatest novel, she manages it by disassociation. If "the girl" is in some way a figure of Kavan's own vulnerability, she's also a cypher, barely glimpsed, and as exasperating as she is pitiable. It's been suggested that the "ice" in *Ice* translates to a junkie's relationship to her drug, yet the book is hardly reducible to this or any other form of allegory. Heroin may be integral to the book, hiding everywhere in plain sight and yet also beside the point. The drama of damage and endurance in *Ice* plays out in an arena of dire necessity and, somehow simultaneously, anomic, dispassionate curiosity.

What makes this not only possible, but also riveting and unforgettable, is Kavan's meticulous, compacted style. The book has the velocity of a thriller yet the causal slippages associated with high modernist writing like Beckett's or Kafka's. The whole presentation is dreamlike, yet even that surface is riven by dream *sequences*, and by anomalous ruptures in point-of-view and narrative momentum. At times this gives the reader the sensation that *Ice* works like a collage or mashup; perhaps William Burroughs has been given a go at it with his scissors and paste pot. By the end, however, one feels at the mercy of an absolutely precise and merciless prose machine, one simply uninterested in producing the illusion of cause and effect. In the place of what's called "plot," Kavan offers up a recursive system, an index of reaction points as unsettling and neatly tailored as a sheaf of Rorschach blots. The book's nearest cousins, it seems to me, are *Crash*, Ballard's most narratively discontinuous and imagistic book, or cinematic contemporaries like Godard's *Alphaville* (released two years before *Ice* but not an influence, probably, on a book in the making many years earlier) and Alain Resnais's *Last Year at Marienbad* (from 1961, and Kavan was an admirer of its screenwriter, the French novelist Alain Robbe-Grillet). It'll stick around, as those have, and it may even cut deeper.

Like the moon, but with sharp edges.

JONATHAN LETHEM

Ice

ONE

I was lost, it was already dusk, I had been driving for hours and was practically out of petrol. The idea of being stranded on these lonely hills in the dark appalled me, so I was glad to see a signpost, and coast down to a garage. When I opened a window to speak to the attendant, the air outside was so cold that I turned up my collar. While he was filling the tank he commented on the weather. "Never known such cold in this month. Forecast says we're in for a real bad freeze-up." Most of my life was spent abroad, soldiering, or exploring remote areas: but although I had just come from the tropics and freeze-ups meant little to me, I was struck by the ominous sound of his words. Anxious to get on, I asked the way to the village I was making for. "You'll never find it in the dark, it's right off the beaten track. And those hill roads are dangerous when they're iced up." He seemed to imply that only a fool would drive on under present conditions, which rather annoyed me. So, cutting short his involved directions, I paid him and drove away, ignoring his last warning shout: "Look out for that ice!"

It had got quite dark by now, and I was soon more hopelessly lost than ever. I knew I should have listened to the fellow, but at the same time wished I had not spoken to him at all. For some unknown reason, his remarks had made me uneasy; they seemed a bad omen for the whole expedition, and I began to regret having embarked on it.

I had been doubtful about the trip all along. I had arrived only the previous day, and should have been attending to things in town instead of visiting friends in the country. I myself did not understand my compulsion to see this girl, who had been in my thoughts all the time I was away, although she was not the reason for my return. I had come back to investigate rumors of a mysterious impending emergency in this part of the world. But as soon as I got here she became an obsession, I could think only of her, felt I must see her immediately, nothing else mattered. Of course I knew it was utterly irrational. And so was my present uneasiness: no harm was likely to come to me in my own country; and yet I was becoming more and more anxious as I drove on.

Reality had always been something of an unknown quantity to me. At times this could be disturbing. Now, for instance, I had visited the girl and her husband before, and kept a vivid recollection of the peaceful, prosperous-looking countryside round their home. But this memory was rapidly fading, losing its reality, becoming increasingly unconvincing and indistinct, as I passed no one on the road, never came to a village, saw no lights anywhere. The sky was black, blacker untended hedges towering against it; and when the headlights occasionally showed roadside buildings, these too were always black, apparently uninhabited and more or less in ruins. It was just as if the entire district had been laid waste during my absence.

I began to wonder if I would ever find her in the general disorder. It did not look as if any organized life could have been going on here since whatever disaster had obliterated the villages and wrecked the farms. As far as I could see, no attempt had been made to restore normality. No rebuilding or work on the land had been done, no animals were in the fields. The road badly needed repairs, the ditches were choked with weeds under the neglected hedges, the whole region appeared to have been left derelict and deserted.

A handful of small white stones hit the windscreen, making me jump. It was so long since I had experienced winter in the north that I failed to recognize the phenomenon. The hail soon turned to snow, diminishing visibility and making driving more difficult. It was bitterly cold, and I became aware of a connection between this fact and my increasing uneasiness. The garage man had said he had never known it so cold at this time, and my own impression was that it was far too early in the season for ice and snow. Suddenly my anxiety was so acute that I wanted to turn and drive back to town; but the road was too narrow, I was forced to follow its interminable windings up and down hill in the lifeless dark. The surface got worse, it got steeper and more slippery all the time. The unaccustomed cold made my head ache as I stared out, straining my eyes in the effort of trying to avoid icy patches, where the car skidded out of control. When the headlights fled over roadside ruins from time to time, the brief glimpse always surprised me, and vanished before I was sure I had really seen it.

An unearthly whiteness began to bloom on the hedges. I passed a gap and glanced through. For a moment, my lights picked out like searchlights the girl's naked body, slight as a child's, ivory white against the dead white of the snow, her hair bright as spun glass. She did not look in my direction. Motionless, she kept her eyes fixed on the walls moving slowly toward her, a glassy, glittering circle of solid ice, of which she was the center. Dazzling flashes came from the ice-cliffs far over her head; below, the outermost fringes of ice had already reached her, immobilized her, set hard as concrete over her feet and ankles. I watched the ice climb higher, covering knees and thighs, saw her mouth open, a black hole in the white face, heard her thin, agonized scream. I felt no pity for her. On the contrary, I derived an indescribable pleasure from seeing her suffer. I disapproved of my own callousness, but there it was. Various factors had combined to produce it, although they were not extenuating circumstances.

I had been infatuated with her at one time, had intended to marry her. Ironically, my aim then had been to shield her from the callousness of the world, which her timidity and fragility seemed to invite. She was over-sensitive, highly strung, afraid of people and life; her personality had been damaged by a sadistic mother who kept her in a permanent state of frightened subjection. The first thing I had to do was to win her trust, so I was always gentle with her, careful to restrain my feelings. She was so thin that, when we danced, I was afraid of hurting her if I held her tightly. Her prominent bones seemed brittle, the protruding wrist-bones had a particular fascination for me. Her hair was astonishing, silver-white, an albino's, sparkling like moonlight, like moonlit venetian glass. I treated her like a glass girl; at times she hardly seemed real. By degrees she lost her fear of me, showed a childish affection, but remained shy and elusive. I thought I had proved to her that I could be trusted, and was content to wait. She seemed on the point of accepting me, although immaturity made it hard to assess the sincerity of her feelings. Her affection perhaps was not altogether pretense, although she deserted me suddenly for the man to whom she was now married.

This was past history. But the consequences of the traumatic experience were still evident in the insomnia and headaches from which I suffered. The drugs prescribed for me produced horrible dreams, in which she always appeared as a helpless victim, her fragile body broken and bruised. These dreams were not confined to sleep only, and a deplorable side effect was the way I had come to enjoy them.

Visibility had improved, the night was no less dark, but the snow had stopped. I could see the remains of a fort on the top of a steep hill. Nothing much was left of it but the tower, it had been gutted, empty window-holes showed like black open mouths. The place seemed vaguely familiar, a distortion of something I half remembered. I seemed to recognize it, thought I had seen it before, but could not be certain, as I had only been here in the summer, when everything looked quite different.

At that time, when I accepted the man's invitation, I suspected him of an ulterior motive in asking me. He was a painter, not serious, a dilettante; one of those people who always have plenty of money without appearing to do any work. Possibly he had a private income: but I suspected him of being something other than what he seemed. The warmth of my reception surprised me, he could not have been more friendly. All the same, I was on my guard.

The girl hardly spoke, stood beside him, glancing sideways at me with big eyes through her long lashes. Her presence affected me strongly, although I scarcely knew in what way. I found it difficult to talk to the two of them. The house was in the middle of a beech wood, so closely surrounded by many tall trees that we seemed to be actually in the treetops, waves of dense green foliage breaking outside every window. I thought of an almost extinct race of large singing lemurs known as the Indris, living in the forest trees of a remote tropical island. The gentle affectionate ways and strange melodious voices of these near-legendary creatures had made a great impression on me, and I began speaking about them, forgetting myself in the fascination of the subject. He appeared interested. She said nothing, and presently left us to see about lunch. The conversation at once became easier when she had gone.

It was midsummer, the weather was very hot, the rustling leaves just outside made a pleasant cool sound. The man's friendliness continued. I seemed to have misjudged him, and began to be embarrassed by my suspicions. He told me he was glad I had come, and went on to speak of the girl. "She's terribly shy and nervous, it does her good to see someone from the outside world. She's too much alone here." I couldn't help wondering how much he knew about me, what she had told him. To remain on the defensive seemed rather absurd; still, there was some reservation in my response to his amiable talk.

I stayed with them for a few days. She kept out of my way. I never saw her unless he was there too. The fine hot weather went on. She wore short, thin, very simple dresses that left her shoulders and arms bare, no stockings, a child's

sandals. In the sunshine her hair dazzled. I knew I would
not be able to forget how she looked. I noted a marked
change in her, a much increased confidence. She smiled
more often, and once in the garden I heard her singing.
When the man called her name she came running. It was
the first time I had seen her happy. Only when she spoke to
me she still showed some constraint. Toward the end of my
visit he asked whether I had talked to her alone. I told him I
had not. He said: "Do have a word with her before you go.
She worries about the past; she's afraid she made you
unhappy." So he knew. She must have told him all there was
to tell. It was not much, certainly. But I would not discuss
what had happened with him and said something evasive.
Tactfully, he changed the subject: but returned to it later on.
"I wish you would set her mind at rest. I shall make an
opportunity for you to speak to her privately." I did not see
how he was going to do this, as the next day was the last I
would spend with them. I was leaving in the late afternoon.

That morning was the hottest there had been. Thunder
was in the air. Even at breakfast time the heat was oppres-
sive. To my surprise, they proposed an outing. I was not to
leave without having seen one of the local beauty spots. A
hill was mentioned, from which there was a celebrated
view: I had heard the name. When I referred to my departure I was told it was only a short drive, and that we should
be back in plenty of time for me to pack my bag. I saw that
they were determined on the arrangement, and agreed.

We took a picnic lunch to eat near the ruins of an old
fort, dating from a remote period when there had been fear
of invasion. The road ended deep in the woods. We left the
car and continued on foot. In the steadily increasing heat, I
refused to hurry, dropped behind, and when I saw the end
of the trees, sat down in the shade. He came back, pulled
me to my feet. "Come along! You'll see that it's worth the
climb." His enthusiasm urged me up a steep sunny slope to
the summit, where I duly admired the view. Still unsatisfied,
he insisted that I must see it from the top of the ruin. He

seemed in a queer state, excitable, almost feverish. In the
dusty dark, I followed him up steps cut inside the tower
wall, his massive figure blocking out the light so that I could
see nothing and might have broken my neck where a step
was missing. There was no parapet at the top, we stood
among heaps of rubble, nothing between us and the drop to
the ground, while he swung his arm, pointing out different
items in the extensive view. "This tower has been a land-
mark for centuries. You can see the whole range of hills
from here. The sea's over there. That's the cathedral spire.
The blue line beyond is the estuary."

I was more interested in closer details: piles of stones,
coils of wire, concrete blocks and other materials for deal-
ing with the coming emergency. Hoping to see something
that would provide a clue to the nature of the expected crisis, I went nearer the edge, looked down at the unprotected
drop at my feet.

"Take care!" he warned, laughing. "You could easily slip
here, or lose your balance. The perfect spot for a murder, I
always think." His laugh sounded so peculiar that I turned
to look at him. He came up to me, saying: "Suppose I give
you a little push . . . like this—" I stepped back just in time,
but missed my footing and stumbled, staggering on to a
crumbling, precarious ledge lower down. His laughing face
hung over me, black against the hot sky. "The fall would
have been an accident, wouldn't it? No witnesses. Only my
word for what happened. Look how unsteady you are on
your feet. Heights seem to affect you." When we got down
to the bottom again I was sweating, my clothes were covered in dust.

The girl had set out the food on the grass in the shade of
an old walnut tree growing there. As usual, she spoke little.
I was not sorry my visit was ending; there was too much
tension in the atmosphere, her proximity was too disturbing. While we were eating I kept glancing at her, at the silvery blaze of hair, the pale, almost transparent skin, the
prominent, brittle wrist-bones. Her husband had lost his

earlier exhilaration and become somewhat morose. He took a sketchbook and wandered off. I did not understand his moods. Heavy clouds appeared in the distance; I felt the humidity in the air and knew there would be a storm before long. My jacket lay on the grass beside me; now I folded it into a cushion, propped it against the tree trunk and rested my head on it. The girl was stretched out full length on the grassy bank just below me, her hands clasped over her forehead, shielding her face from the glare. She kept quite still, without speaking, her raised arms displaying the slight roughness and darkness of the shaved armpits, where tiny drops of sweat sparkled like frost. The thin dress she was wearing showed the slight curves of her childish body: I could see that she wore nothing underneath it.

She was crouching in front of me, a little lower down the slope, her flesh less white than the snow. Great ice-cliffs were closing in on all sides. The light was fluorescent, a cold flat shadowless icelight. No sun, no shadows, no life, a dead cold. We were in the center of the advancing circle. I had to try to save her. I called: "Come up here—quick!" She turned her head, but without moving, her hair glinting like tarnished silver in the flat light. I went down to her, said: "Don't be so frightened. I promise I'll save you. We must get to the top of the tower." She seemed not to understand, perhaps did not hear because of the rumbling roar of the approaching ice. I got hold of her, pulled her up the slope: it was easy, she was almost weightless. Outside the ruin I stopped, holding her with one arm, looked round and saw at once that it was useless to go any higher. The tower was bound to fall; it would collapse, and be pulverized instantly under millions of tons of ice. The cold scorched my lungs, the ice was so near. She was shivering violently, her shoulders were ice already; I held her closer to me, wrapped both arms round her tight.

Little time was left, but at least we would share the same end. Ice had already engulfed the forest, the last ranks of trees were splintering. Her silver hair touched my mouth, she was leaning against me. Then I lost her; my hands could not find her again. A snapped-off tree trunk was dancing high in the sky, hurled up hundreds of feet by the impact of the ice. There was a flash, everything was shaken. My suitcase was lying open, half-packed, on the bed. The windows of my room were still wide open, the curtains streamed into the room. Outside the treetops were streaming, the sky had gone dark. I saw no rain, but thunder still rolled and echoed, and as I looked out lightning flashed again. The temperature had fallen several degrees since morning. I hurried to put on my jacket and shut the window.

I had been following the right road, after all. After running like a tunnel between unpruned hedges that met overhead, it wound through the dark beech wood to end in front of the house. No light was visible. The place looked derelict, uninhabited, like the others I had passed. I sounded the horn several times and waited. It was late, they might be in bed. If she was there I had to see her, and that was all there was to it. After some delay, the man came and let me in. He did not seem pleased to see me this time, which was understandable if I had woken him up. He appeared to be in his dressing-gown.

The house was without electricity. He went first, flashing a torch. I kept my coat on, although the living-room fire gave out some warmth. In the lamplight I was surprised to see how much he had altered while I had been abroad. He looked heavier, harder, tougher; the amiable expression had gone. It was not a dressing-gown he was wearing, but the long overcoat of some uniform, which made him seem unfamiliar. My old suspicions revived; here was someone who was cashing in on the emergency before it had even arrived. His face did not appear friendly. I apologized for coming so late, explaining that I had lost my way. He was in the process of getting drunk. Bottles and glasses stood on a small table. "Well, here's to your arrival." There was no cordiality in his manner or in his voice, which had a sardonic tone that was new. He poured me a drink and sat down, the long

overcoat draping his knees. I looked for the bulging pocket,
the protruding butt, but nothing of the sort was visible
under the coat. We sat drinking together. I made conversation about my travels, waiting for the girl to appear. There
was no sign of her; not a sound from the rest of the house.
He did not mention her, and I could tell that he refrained
deliberately by his look of malicious amusement. The room
I remembered as charming was now neglected, dirty. Plaster had fallen from the ceiling, there were deep cracks in the
walls as from the effect of blast, black patches where rain
had seeped in, and with it, the devastation outside. When
my impatience became uncontrollable I asked how she was.
"She's dying." He grinned spitefully at my exclamation. "As
we all are." It was his idea of a joke at my expense. I saw
that he meant to prevent our meeting.

I needed to see her; it was vital. I said: "I'll go now and
leave you in peace. But could you give me something to eat
first? I've had nothing since midday." He went out and in a
rough overbearing voice shouted to her to bring food. The
destruction outside was contagious and had infected everything, including their relationship, and the appearance of
the room. She brought a tray with bread and butter, a plate
of ham, and I looked closely to see if her appearance had
changed too. She only looked thinner than ever, and more
nearly transparent. She was completely silent, and seemed
frightened, withdrawn, as she had been when I knew her
first. I longed to ask questions, to talk to her alone, but was
not given the chance. The man watched us all the time as he
went on drinking. Alcohol made him quarrelsome; he got
angry when I refused to drink any more, determined to pick
a quarrel with me. I knew I ought to go, but my head ached
abominably and made me reluctant to move. I kept pressing
my hand over my eyes and forehead. Evidently the girl
noticed this, for she left the room for a minute, came back
with something in the palm of her hand, murmured: "An
aspirin for your head." Like a bully, he shouted: "What are
you whispering to him?" Touched by her thought for me, I

would have liked to do more than thank her; but his scowl was so vicious that I got up to leave.

He did not come to see me off. I felt my way through the darkness by walls and furniture, faced a pale shimmer of snow when I opened the outer door. It was so cold that I hurriedly shut myself in the car and put on the heater. Looking up from the dashboard, I heard her call softly something of which I caught only the words "promise" and "don't forget." I switched on the headlights, saw her in the doorway, thin arms clasped round her chest. Her face wore its victim's look, which was of course psychological, the result of injuries she had received in childhood; I saw it as the faintest possible hint of bruising on the extremely delicate, fine, white skin in the region of eyes and mouth. It was madly attractive to me in a certain way. I had barely caught sight of it now before the car began moving; I was automatically pressing the starter, not expecting it to work in the freezing cold. At the same moment, in what I took for an optical delusion, the black interior of the house prolonged itself into a black arm and hand, which shot out and grasped her so violently that her shocked white face cracked to pieces and she tumbled into the dark.

I could not get over the deterioration in their relationship. While she was happy I had dissociated myself, been outside the situation. Now I felt implicated, involved with her again.

TWO

I heard that the girl had left home suddenly. No one knew where she was. The husband thought she might have gone abroad. It was only a guess. He had no information. I was agitated and asked endless questions, but no concrete facts emerged. "I know no more than you. She simply vanished, I suppose she's entitled to go if she wants to—she's free, white and twenty-one." He adopted a facetious tone, I could not tell if he was speaking the truth. The police did not suspect foul play. There was no reason to think harm had come to her, or that she had not gone away voluntarily. She was old enough to know her own mind. People were constantly disappearing; hundreds left home and were not seen again, many of them women unhappily married. Her marriage was known to have been breaking up. Almost certainly she was better off now, and only wanted to be left in peace. Further investigation would be resented and lead to more trouble.

This was a convenient view for them, it excused them from taking action. But I did not accept it. She had been conditioned into obedience since early childhood, her independence destroyed by systematic suppression. I did not believe her capable of taking such a drastic step on her own initiative: I suspected pressure from outside. I wished I could talk to someone who knew her well, but she seemed to have had no close friends.

The husband came to town on some mysterious business, and I asked him to lunch at my club. We talked for two hours, but in the end I was none the wiser. He persistently treated the whole affair lightly, said he was glad she had gone. "Her neurotic behavior nearly drove *me* demented. I'd had all I could take. She refused to see a psychiatrist. Finally she walked out on me without a word. No explanation. No warning." He spoke as if he was the injured party. "She went her own way without considering me, so I'm not worrying about her. She won't come back, that's one thing certain." While he was away from home, I took the opportunity of driving down to the house and going through the things in her room, but found nothing in the way of a clue. There was just the usual collection of pathetic rubbish: a china bird; a broken string of fake pearls; snapshots in an old chocolate box. One of these, in which a lake reflected perfectly her face and her shining hair, I put into my wallet.

Somehow or other I had to find her; the fact remained. I felt the same compulsive urge that had driven me straight to the country when I first arrived. There was no rational explanation, I could not account for it. It was a sort of craving that had to be satisfied.

I abandoned all my own affairs. From now on my business was to search for her. Nothing else mattered. Certain sources of possible information were still available. Hairdressers. Clerks who kept records of transport bookings. Those fringe characters. I went to the places such people frequented, stood about playing the fruit machines until I saw a chance of speaking. Money helped. So did intuition. No clue was too slender to follow up. The approaching emergency made it all the more urgent to find her quickly. I could not get her out of my head. I had not seen all the things I remembered about her. During my first visit I was in their living-room, talking about the Indris, my favorite subject. The man listened. She went to and fro arranging flowers. On an impulse I said the pair of them resembled the lemurs, both so friendly and charming, and living together so happily here in the trees. He laughed. She looked horrified and ran out through the French window, silvery hair floating behind her, her bare legs flashing pale. The secret, shady garden, hidden away in seclusion and silence, was a pleasant cool retreat from the heat of summer. Then suddenly it was unnaturally, fearfully cold. The masses of dense foliage all around became prison walls, impassable circular green ice-walls, surging toward her; just before they closed in, I caught the terrified glint of her eyes.

On a winter day she was in the studio, posing for him in the nude, her arms raised in a graceful position. To hold it for any length of time must have been a strain, I wondered how she managed to keep so still; until I saw the cords attached to her wrists and ankles. The room was cold. There was thick frost on the window panes and snow piled up on the sill outside. He wore the long uniform coat. She was shivering. When she asked, "May I have a rest?" her voice had a pathetic tremor. He frowned, looked at his watch before he put down his palette. "All right. That'll do for now. You can dress." He untied her. The cords had left deep red angry rings on the white flesh. Her movements were slow and clumsy from cold, she fumbled awkwardly with buttons, suspenders. This seemed to annoy him, He turned away from her sharply, his face irritable. She kept glancing nervously at him, her mouth was unsteady, her hands would not stop shaking.

Another time the two were together in a cold room. As usual, he wore the long coat. It was night, freezing hard. He had a book in his hand, she was doing nothing. She looked cold and miserable, huddled up in a thick gray loden coat with a red and blue check lining. The room was silent and full of tension. It could be felt that neither of them had spoken for a long time. Outside the window, a twig snapped in the iron frost with a sound like a handclap. He dropped the book and got up to put on a record. Instantly she began to protest. "Oh, no! Not that awful singing, for heaven's sake!" He ignored her, went on with what he was doing. The turntable started revolving. It was a record I had given them from my tape recording of the lemurs' song. To me, the extraordinary jungle music was lovely, mysterious, magical.

To her it was a sort of torture, apparently. She covered her ears with her hands, winced at the high notes, looked more and more distraught. When the record ended and he restarted it without a moment's pause, she cried out as if he had struck her, "No! I won't listen to it all over again!" threw herself at the mechanism, stopped it so abruptly that the voices expired in uncanny wailing. He faced her angrily. "What the hell do you think you're doing? Have you gone off your head?" "You know I can't stand that horrible record." She seemed almost beside herself. "You only play it because I hate it so much . . ." Tears sprang unchecked from her eyes, she brushed them away carelessly with her hand.

He glared at her, said: "Why should I sit in silence for hours just because you don't choose to open your mouth?" His angry voice was full of indignant resentment. "What's wrong with you, anyhow, these days? Why can't you behave like a normal being?" She did not answer, dropped her face in her hands. Tears dripped between her fingers. He gazed at her with a disgusted expression. "I might as well be in solitary confinement as alone with you here. But I warn you I'm not going to put up with it much longer. I've had enough. I'm sick and tired of the way you're carrying on. Pull yourself together, or else—" With a threatening scowl, he went out, banging the door behind him. A silence followed, while she stood like a lost child, tears wet on her cheeks. Next she started wandering aimlessly round the room, stopped by the window, pulled the curtain aside, then cried out in amazement.

Instead of the darkness, she faced a stupendous sky-conflagration, an incredible glacial dream-scene. Cold coruscations of rainbow fire pulsed overhead, shot through by shafts of pure incandescence thrown out by mountains of solid ice towering all around. Closer, the trees round the house, sheathed in ice, dripped and sparkled with weird prismatic jewels, reflecting the vivid changing cascades above. Instead of the familiar night sky, the aurora borealis formed a blazing, vibrating roof of intense cold and color, beneath which the earth was trapped with all its inhabitants, walled in by those impassable glittering ice-cliffs. The world had become an arctic prison from which no escape was possible, all its creatures trapped as securely as were the trees, already lifeless inside their deadly resplendent armor.

Despairingly she looked all around. She was completely encircled by the tremendous ice walls, which were made fluid by explosions of blinding light, so that they moved and changed with a continuous liquid motion, advancing in torrents of ice, avalanches as big as oceans, flooding everywhere over the doomed world. Wherever she looked, she saw the same fearful encirclement, soaring battlements of ice, an overhanging ring of frigid, fiery, colossal waves about to collapse upon her. Frozen by the deathly cold emanating from the ice, dazzled by the blaze of crystalline ice-light, she felt herself becoming part of the polar vision, her structure becoming one with the structure of ice and snow. As her fate, she accepted the world of ice, shining, shimmering, dead; she resigned herself to the triumph of glaciers and the death of her world.

It was essential for me to find her without delay. The situation was alarming, the atmosphere tense, the emergency imminent. There was talk of a secret act of aggression by some foreign power, but no one knew what had actually happened. The government would not disclose the facts. I was informed privately of a steep rise in radioactive pollution, pointing to the explosion of a nuclear device, but of an unknown type, the consequences of which could not be accurately predicted. It was possible that polar modifications had resulted, and would lead to a substantial climatic change due to the refraction of solar heat. If the melting Antarctic ice cap flowed over the South Pacific and Atlantic oceans, a vast ice-mass would be created, reflecting the sun's rays and throwing them back into outer space, thus depriving the earth of warmth. In town, everything was chaotic and contradictory. News from abroad was censored, but travel was left unrestricted. Confusion was increased by a spate of new and conflicting regulations, and by the arbitrary way controls were imposed or lifted. The one thing that would have clarified the position was an overall picture of world events; but this was prohibited by the determination of the politicians to ban all foreign news. My impression was that they had lost their heads, did not know how to deal with the approaching danger, and hoped to keep the public in ignorance of its exact nature until a plan had been evolved.

No doubt people would have been more concerned, and would have made greater efforts to find out what was taking place in other countries, if, at home, they had not been obliged to contend with the fuel shortage, the power cuts, the breakdown of transport, and the rapid diversion of supplies to the black market.

There was no sign of a break in the abnormal cold. My room was reasonably warm, but even in hotels heating was being reduced to a minimum, and, outside, the erratic, restricted services hampered my investigations. The river had been frozen over for weeks, the total paralysis of the docks was a serious problem. All essential commodities were in short supply; rationing, at least of fuel and food, could not be delayed much longer, despite the reluctance of those in power to resort to unpopular measures.

Everyone who could do so was leaving in search of better conditions. No more passages were available, either by sea or air; there were long waiting lists for all ships and planes. I had no proof that the girl was already abroad. On the whole it seemed unlikely she would have managed to leave the country, and an obscure train of thought suggested that she might embark on a certain vessel.

The port was a long way off, to reach it involved a long complicated journey. I was delayed, got there, after traveling all night, only an hour before sailing time. The passengers were already aboard, crowding the decks with friends who were seeing them off. The first thing I had to do was to speak to the captain. He turned out to be maddeningly talkative. While I became more and more impatient, he complained at great length about the way the authorities allowed overcrowding: it was a danger to his ship, unfair to himself, to the company, the passengers, the insurance people. That was his business. As soon as I got permission to get on with my own, I made a methodical search of the ship, but without finding a trace of the person I wanted.

Finally I gave up in despair and went out on deck. Too tired and disheartened to push through the crowds of people milling about there, I stood by the rail, overcome by a sudden urge to abandon the whole affair. I had never really had a valid reason for supposing the girl would be on this ship. Suddenly it seemed neither sensible, nor even sane, to continue search based solely on vague surmise; particularly as my attitude to its object was so undefined. When I considered that imperative need I felt for her, as for a missing part of myself, it appeared less like love than an inexplicable aberration, the sign of some character flaw I ought to eradicate, instead of letting it dominate me.

At this moment a big black-backed gull sailed past, almost brushing my cheek with its wing tip, as if on purpose to draw my attention and eyes after it up to the boat deck. At once I saw her there, looking away from me, where no one had been before; and everything I had just been thinking was swept out of my head by a wave of excitement, my old craving for her returned. I was convinced it was she without even seeing her face; no other girl in the world had such dazzling hair, or was so thin that her fragility could be seen through a thick gray coat. I simply had to reach her, it was all I could think of. Envying the gull's effortless flight, I plunged straight into the solid mass of humanity separating me from her, and forced my way through. I had hardly any time, in a moment the boat would be sailing. Visitors were leaving already, forming a strong cross current I had to fight. My one idea was to get to the boat deck before it

was too late. In my anxiety, I must have pushed people
aside. Hostile remarks were made, a fist shaken. I tried to
explain my urgency to those who obstructed me, but they
would not listen. Three tough-looking young men linked
arms and aggressively barred my way, their expressions
threatening. I had not meant to offend, hardly knew what I
was doing. I was thinking only of her. Suddenly an official voice shouted through a loudspeaker: "All visitors
ashore! The gangway will be raised in exactly two minutes." The ship's siren sounded an ear-splitting blast. An
immediate rush followed. It was quite impossible to resist
the human flood surging toward the gangway. I was caught
up in the stampede, dragged along with it, off the boat, and
on to the quay.

Standing at the water's edge, I soon saw her high above
me, considerably further off now. The ship had already
moved away from the shore and was gathering speed every
second, already divided from me by a strip of water too
wide to jump. In desperation, I shouted and waved my
arms, trying to attract her attention. It was hopeless. A
whole sea of arms waved all around me, innumerable voices
were shouting unintelligibly. I saw her turn to speak to
somebody who had just joined her, at the same time pulling
a hood over her head, so that her hair was hidden. Immediate doubts invaded me, and increased as I watched her.
After all, perhaps she was not the right girl; she seemed too
self-possessed. But I was not certain.

The boat was now beginning the turn that would bring it
round facing the mouth of the harbor, leaving behind it a
curving track of smoother water, like the swath left by a
scythe. I stood staring after it, although cold had driven the
passengers off the decks and there was no more hope of recognition. I dimly remembered what I had been thinking just
before I caught sight of her, but only as one might recall an
incident from a dream. Once again the urgency of the
search had reclaimed me; I was totally absorbed in that

obsessional need, as for a lost, essential portion of my own
being. Everything else in the world seemed immaterial.

All around me people were walking away, stamping their
feet in the cold. I hardly noticed the mass departure. It did
not occur to me to leave the edge of the water, over which I
continued to gaze at the vessel's diminishing shape. I had
been an utter fool. I was furious with myself for letting it go
without discovering the identity of the girl on board. Now I
would never be sure whether she had, or had not, been the
right one. And if she had been, how would I ever find her
again? A mournful hoot traveled across the water: the ship
was leaving the protection of the harbor, heading out into
the open sea. Already meeting the offshore rollers, it kept
disappearing behind gray masses of water surging along the
horizon. It looked absurdly small, a toy boat. I lost sight of
it, my eyes could not find it again. It was lost irretrievably.

I only became aware that everyone else had gone and that
I was alone there, when two policemen approached, marching along side by side, and pointed to a sign, "Loitering on
the waterfront strictly forbidden: War Department." "Why
are you hanging about here? Can't you read?" Needless to
say, they refused to believe that I had not seen it. Hugely tall
in their helmets, they stood on each side, so close that their
guns stuck into me, and demanded my papers. These were
in order. There was nothing against me. Nevertheless, my
conduct had been suspicious, they insisted on writing down
my name and address. Again I had acted stupidly, this time
by drawing attention to myself. Now that my name had
been noted, it would appear in the records; I would be
known to the police everywhere, my movements would be
kept under observation. It would be a serious handicap in
my search.

As the two men hustled me through the gates, something
made me look up at a row of big black-backed gulls perched
on a wall, all facing into the wind and pointing out to sea,
as motionless as if they had been stuffed and put up there to

act as a message. On the spot I decided to leave the country before any of my visas lapsed or were canceled. No particular place seemed more or less promising than another as a base from which to start searching. But to attempt to operate from here while under suspicion would surely invite failure.

I had to leave at once, before the police report circulated. It could not have been done through the normal channels. By employing other methods, I managed to board a northbound cargo boat carrying a few passengers, and booked to the end of the voyage. The purser was willing to vacate his cabin for a consideration. Next day, at the first port of the trip, I went on deck to watch our arrival. I remembered the complaints I had been forced to listen to about overcrowding when I saw a lot of people packed together on the deck below, waiting to disembark. Twelve was the authorized number of passengers. I wondered how many more were on board.

It was extremely cold. Loose fragments of pack ice drifted past in the green water. Everything was misty and indistinct. The landing-stage was quite close, but the buildings at the end of the jetty looked insubstantial, amorphous. A girl in a heavy gray coat with a hood was standing a little apart from the other passengers, leaning on the rail. Occasionally a fold of the coat would blow back, showing a quilted check lining. It was the coat I noticed; although I knew perfectly well that such coats had become almost a uniform among women since the start of the cold, and were to be seen everywhere.

The mist began to lift and break up, the sun would shine later. A rugged coastline appeared with many inlets and jagged rocks, snow-covered mountains behind. There were many small islands, some of which floated up and became clouds, while formations of cloud or mist descended and anchored themselves in the sea. The white snowy landscape below, and above the canopy of misty white light, the effect of an oriental painting, nothing solid about it. The town appeared to consist of ruins collapsing on one another in shapeless disorder, a town of sandcastles, wrecked by the tide. A great wall which had protected it was broken in many places, both ends subsiding uselessly into the water. The place had once been important. Its fortifications had lain in ruins for centuries. It was still of some historical interest.

Sudden silence fell. The engines had stopped. The boat was still moving forward under its own momentum. I heard the faint swish of water against the sides, the plangent crying of sea birds, that sad northern sound. Otherwise all was silent. No sounds of traffic, of bells or voices, came from the land. The town of ruins waited in utter silence under the brooding mountains. I thought of long narrow ancient ships, vast collections of loot preserved in barrows, winged helmets, drinking horns, great heavy ornaments of gold and silver, piles of fossilized bones. It looked a place of the past, of the dead.

There was a shout from the bridge. On the jetty a group of sullen-faced men rose out of the ground. They were armed and wore uniform: black padded tunics, belted tight at the waist, high boots, fur caps. The knives in their belts caught the light as they moved. They looked outlandish, even menacing. I heard somebody say they were the warden's men, which meant nothing; I had not heard of this warden. Their presence surprised me since private armies were forbidden by law. Ropes were thrown; they caught them and made them fast. The gangway crashed down. A slight stir started among the passengers, who picked up luggage, got out passports and papers, began a slow shuffling progress toward a barrier that had been set up.

Only the girl in the gray coat did not concern herself with landing, did not change her position. As the others moved forward and she was left isolated, my interest increased, I could not detach my attention from her, kept on watching. What most struck me was her complete stillness. Such a passive attitude, suggesting both resistance and resignation, did not seem entirely normal in a young girl. She could not have been more motionless if she had been tied to the rail, and I thought how easily bonds could be hidden by the voluminous coat.

A bright strand of glittering blonde hair, almost white, escaped from the hood and blew loose in the wind; I felt a sudden excitement; but reminded myself that many northerners were extremely fair. All the same, my interest now became compelling, I was longing to see her face. She would have to look up toward me before that could happen.

The passengers' forward movement was interrupted. Men in uniform came aboard and cleared a way through them, demanding room for the warden, shouting peremptory orders. Space was made for a tall man, yellow haired, handsome in a tough, hawk-hard northern fashion, his height jutting above those near him. His arrogant manner, his total disregard for the feelings of others, made an unpleasant impression. As if he sensed my criticism, he glanced up for a second. His eyes were startling pieces of bright blue ice. I saw that he was making for the girl in the gray coat, the one person who had not seen him. Everyone else was staring. When he called out, "Why are you standing there? Have you gone to sleep?" she swung round as if terribly startled. "Hurry up! The car's waiting." He went close and touched her. He was smiling, but I detected a hint of a threat in his voice and behavior. She hung back, seemed unwilling to go with him. He linked arms with her, apparently friendly, but really forcing her forward against her will, pulling her along with him through the bunched, staring people. She still did not look up, I could not see her expression, but I could imagine his iron grip on her thin wrist. They left the ship before anyone else, and were immediately driven off in a big black car.

I had been standing there as if petrified. Suddenly now I made a decision. It seemed worth taking a chance. Although without having seen her face . . . I had no other clue to follow, in any case.

I ran down to the cabin, sent for the purser, told him I had changed my plans. "I'm going ashore here." He looked at me as though I was out of my mind. "Please yourself." He shrugged his shoulders indifferently, but could not quite conceal an incipient grin. He had already received his money. Now he would be able to collect a second payment from somebody else for the remainder of the voyage.

I hurriedly threw into my suitcase the few things I had unpacked.

THREE

Carrying my suitcase, I walked into the town. Silence obtruded itself. Nothing moved. The devastation was even greater than it had seemed from the boat. Not a building intact. Wreckage heaped in blank spaces where houses had been. Walls had crumbled; steps ascended and stopped in mid-air; arches opened on to deep craters. Little had been done to repair this wholesale destruction. Only the main streets were clear of rubble, the rest obliterated. Faint tracks, like the tracks of animals, but made by human beings, twisted among the debris. I looked in vain for somebody to direct me. The whole place seemed deserted. A train whistle at last guided me to the station, a small makeshift building constructed with materials salvaged from ruins, which reminded me of a discarded film set. Even here there was no sign of life, although presumably a train had just left. It was hard to believe the place was really in use; that anything really functioned. I was aware of an uncertainty of the real, in my surroundings and in myself. What I saw had no solidity, it was all made of mist and nylon, with nothing behind.

I went on to the platform. They must have dynamited some of the ruins to lay the track. I could see the single line running out of the town, crossing a strip of open ground before it entered the fir forest. This fragile link with the world did not inspire confidence. I had the feeling it stopped just beyond the first trees. The mountains rose close behind. I shouted, "Is anyone here?" A man appeared from somewhere, made a threatening gesture. "You're trespassing—get out!" I explained

that I had just come off the boat and wanted to find a room.
He stared, hostile, suspicious, uncouth, saying nothing. I asked
the way to the main street. In a sulky voice I could hardly
understand he muttered a few words, staring at me the whole
time as if I had dropped from Mars.

I walked on with my bag, came to an open square where
people were going about. The men's black tunics were vari-
ations of those I had already seen, and most of the wearers
carried knives or guns. The women also wore black, producing a gloomy effect. All the faces were blank and unsmil-
ing. For the first time I saw signs that some buildings were
occupied, a few even had glass in the windows. There were
market stalls and small shops: wooden huts and lean-tos
had been tacked on to some of the patched-up ruins. A café
was open at the end of the square, and there was a cinema,
shut, displaying a tattered advertisement of a year-old pro-
gram. This evidently was the living heart of the town; the
rest was just the remains of the dead past.

I invited the proprietor of the café to drink with me, hoping to establish good relations before I asked for a room. All
these people seemed insular and suspicious, antagonistic to
strangers. We drank the local brandy made out of plums,
potent and fiery, a good drink for a cold climate. He was a
big, robust man, better than a peasant. At first I could
hardly get a word out of him, but over the second glass he
relaxed enough to ask why I had come. "Nobody ever
comes here; we have nothing to attract foreigners—only
ruins." I said: "The ruins of your town are famous. They're
the reason for my coming. I'm making a study of them for a
learned society." I had decided beforehand to say this. "You
mean people in other countries are interested?" "Certainly.
This town is a place of historic importance." He was flattered, as I expected. "That's true. We have a glorious war
record." "And also a record of discovery. Did you know
that a map has been found recently which indicates that
your long boats crossed the Atlantic and were the first to
reach the new world?" "You expect to find proof of this in

the ruins?" It had not occurred to me, but I assented. "I know of course that I must get permits: everything must be done correctly. Unfortunately I don't know who's the right man to approach." Without hesitation he said: "You must ask the warden. He controls everything." Here was an unexpected stroke of luck. "How do I get in touch with him?" I had a vision of an iron hand gripping a girl's thin wrist, crushing the brittle prominent bones. "That's simple. You make an appointment through one of the secretaries at the High House." I was delighted by such good fortune. I had been prepared to wait and scheme for a chance of seeing this man; now the opportunity had presented itself at the very beginning.

The business of the room was also settled without difficulty. I was having a run of good luck. Although the proprietor could not accommodate me himself, his sister who lived nearby had a spare room I could rent. "She's a widow and can do with the extra money, you understand." He went off to telephone to her; returned after rather a long absence, saying that it was all arranged. He would provide my two main meals at the café; breakfast would be brought to my room. "You won't be disturbed there while you're working, it's very quiet. The house looks away from the street, faces the water; and nobody ever goes *there*." His cooperation was valuable, so to keep the conversation going I asked why people avoided the vicinity of the fjord. "Because they're afraid of the dragon that lives at the bottom." I looked at him, thought he was joking; but his face was perfectly serious, his voice had been matter-of-fact. I had never before met anyone who owned a telephone and believed in dragons. It amused me, and also contributed to my sense of the unreal.

The room proved to be dark and devoid of comfort or convenience. It was not warm enough. However, it had a bed, a table and chair—the basic necessities. I was lucky to get it as no other accommodation was available. The sister looked older and much less sophisticated than her brother, who must have persuaded her to take me in against her will during their long talk on the telephone. She was evidently reluctant to admit a foreigner to the house where she lived alone; I could feel her suspicious dislike. To avoid trouble I paid the exorbitant price she asked without question, a week in advance.

I asked for the keys, saying I would have a duplicate cut for the outer door: I had to be independent. She brought the two keys, but gave me only the key of my own door, hiding the other one in the palm of her hand. I told her to hand it over. She refused. I insisted. She became stubborn and retreated into the kitchen. I followed and took the key from her forcibly. I did not much care for this sort of behavior, but a principle was involved. She would not oppose me again.

I went out and walked about, exploring the town: the empty lanes silent between shapeless shapes of decay, the ruined forts jutting into the greengage sea, the huge slab-steps of a giant's staircase where the great wall had fallen, subsiding in solid sections. Everywhere the ubiquitous ruins, decayed fortifications, evidences of a warlike bloodthirsty past. I searched for buildings of a more recent date. There were none. The dwindling population lived like rats in the ruins of a lost martial supremacy. If one place became uninhabitable its occupants moved to another. The community was gradually dying out, each year its numbers declined. There were enough disintegrating structures to last them out. At first it was hard to distinguish the inhabited buildings; I learned to look for the signs of occupation, the reinforced door, the boarded-up windows.

I made an appointment to see the warden at the High House, which dominated the town, a fortress-like mass built at its highest point. At the time agreed, I climbed a steep road, the only one that led to it. From the outside the place looked like an armed fort, enormously massive, thick walls, no windows, some narrow slits high up that might have been meant for machine guns. Batteries flanked the entrance, apparently trained on the road. I assumed they were relics of some old campaign, although they did not look especially obsolete. I had spoken to a secretary on the telephone; but now I was met by four armed guards in black tunics, who escorted me down a long corridor, two walking in front, two behind. It was dark. High above, thin pencils of daylight, entering through the slits in the outer wall, dimly revealed glimpses of other corridors, galleries, stairs, bridge-like landings, at different levels, radiating in different directions. The invisible ceiling must have been enormously high, the full height of the building, for all these indistinct ramifications were far overhead. Something moved at the end of one vista: a girl's figure. I rushed after her as she started to climb some stairs, her silvery hair lifting, glimmering in the darkness, at every step.

The short steep stair led to one room only, large, sparsely furnished, its polished floor bare like a dance floor. I was immediately struck by the unnatural silence, a curious hushed quality in the air, which reduced her movements to mouse-like scratchings. Not a sound penetrated from outside or from other parts of the building. I was puzzled, until it dawned on me that the room had been soundproofed, so that whatever took place there would be inaudible beyond its four walls. Then it at once became obvious why this particular room had been allotted to her.

She was in bed, not asleep, waiting. A faint pinkish glow came from a lamp beside her. The wide bed stood on a platform, bed and platform alike covered in sheepskin, facing a great mirror nearly as long as the wall. Alone here, where nobody could hear her, where nobody was *meant* to hear, she was cut off from all contact, totally vulnerable, at the mercy of the man who came in without knocking, without a word, his cold, very bright blue eyes pouncing on hers in the glass. She crouched motionless, staring silently into the mirror, as if mesmerized. The hypnotic power of his eyes could destroy her will, already weakened by the mother who for years had persistently crushed it into submission. Forced since childhood into a victim's pattern of thought and behavior, she was defenseless against his aggressive will, which was able to take complete possession of her. I saw it happen.

He approached the bed with unhurried steps. She did not move until he bent over her, when she twisted away abruptly, as if trying to escape, buried her face in the pillow. His hand reached out, slid over her shoulder, strong fingers feeling along her jawbone, gripping, tilting, forcing her head up. She resisted violently, in sudden terror, twisting and turning wildly, struggling against his strength. He did nothing at all, let her go on fighting. Her feeble struggles amused him, he knew they would not last long. He looked on in silence, in half-smiling amusement, always tilting her face with slight but inescapable pressure, while she exhausted herself.

Suddenly she gave in, worn out, beaten; she was panting, her face was wet. He tightened his grip slightly, compelled her to look straight at him. To bring the thing to a finish, he stared into her dilated eyes, implacably forced into them his own arrogant, ice-blue gaze. This was the moment of her surrender; opposition collapsed at this point, when she seemed to fall and drown in those cold blue mesmeric depths. Now she had no more will. He could do what he liked with her.

He leaned further, knelt on the bed, pushed her down with his hands on her shoulders. Will-less, she submitted to him, even to the extent of making small compliant movements fitting her body to his. She was dazed, she hardly knew what was happening, her normal state of consciousness interrupted, lost, the nature of her surrender not understood. He was intent only on his enjoyment.

Later she did not move, gave no indication of life, lying exposed on the ruined bed as on a slab in a mortuary. Sheets and blankets spilled on to the floor, trailed over the edge of the dais. Her head hung over the edge of the bed in a slightly unnatural position, the neck slightly twisted in a way that suggested violence, the bright hair twisted into a sort of rope by his hands. He sat with his hand upon her, asserting his right to his prey. When his fingers passed over her naked body, lingering on thighs and breasts, she was shaken by a long painful shudder; then she went still again.

He lifted her head with one hand, looked into her face for a moment, let the head fall back on the pillow; it lay as it fell. He stood up, moved away from the bed; his foot caught in the fold of a blanket, he kicked it back and went on to the door. He had not spoken a single word since he entered the room, and he left it without a sound, apart from the faint click of the closing door. To her, this silence was one of the most terrifying things about him, in some way associated with his power over her.

I wondered where I was being taken. The place was colossal, the passages wound on and on. We passed the trap doors of oubliettes, cells hacked out of the rock. The walls of these hutches were running with water, with some noisome exudation. Perilous steps led down to still deeper dungeons. We went through several pairs of huge doors, which the guards in front unlocked and the others slammed shut behind us.

The warden received me in a civilized room. It was spacious and well-proportioned, the wood floor reflecting dim old chandeliers. The windows faced away from the town, over park-like grounds, sloping down to the distant fjord. His perfectly fitting black tunic was of superb material, his high boots shone like mirrors. He was wearing the colored ribbon of some order I did not know. This time my impression was more favorable; the arrogant look I disliked was less in evidence, although it was clear that he was a born ruler, a law unto himself, not to be judged by the usual standards. "What can I do for you?" He greeted me with formal politeness, his blue eyes looked me straight in the face. I told him the story I had prepared. He agreed at once to have the necessary permits made out and signed, I would get them tomorrow. On his own initiative he suggested adding a note to the effect that I was to be given help in my investigations. To me it seemed superfluous. He said: "You don't know these people. They are naturally lawless and have an innate dislike of strangers, their ways are violent and archaic. I've tried hard to introduce more modern attitudes. But it's useless, they're embedded in the past like Lot's wife in her pillar of salt; you can't detach them from it." I thanked him; at the same time I was thinking about the guards, who hardly seemed to fit in with his enlightened outlook.

He remarked that I had chosen a strange time for my visit. I asked why. "The ice will be here very soon. The harbor will freeze, we shall be cut off." He flashed a blue glance at me. Something had not been said. He had a trick of blinking his very bright eyes, which then seemed to emit blue flames. He went on: "You may be stranded here longer than you bargained for." Again the sharp look, as if something more were implied. I told him: "I'm only staying for a week or so. I don't expect to find anything new. It's more a matter of getting the atmosphere." In spite of my original aversion, I suddenly had a curious sense of contact with him, almost as though some personal link existed between us. The feeling was so unexpected, unaccountable and confusing that I added, "Please don't misunderstand me," without knowing quite what I meant. He seemed gratified, smiled, and at once became more friendly. "So we speak the same language. Good. I'm glad you've come. We need closer contact in this country with the sophisticated nations. This is a beginning." Still somewhat hazy as to what we were talking about, I stood up to go, thanking him again. He shook my hand. "You must come and dine one evening. Let me know in the meantime if I can be of any further service to you."

I was jubilant. My luck was holding. I seemed almost to have attained my object already, I was sure of a chance of seeing the girl. If the dinner invitation failed to materialize, I could always fall back on his final offer.

FOUR

The signed permits arrived the next day. The warden had initialed an additional sentence saying that I was to receive every assistance. This impressed the café proprietor, and I left it to him to circulate the message.

I began making notes on the town: my performance had to be convincing and thorough. I had sometimes thought vaguely of writing about the fascinating singing lemurs; now I had a perfect opportunity to describe them before the memory faded. Each day I wrote a little about my surroundings and a lot more on the other subject. There was nothing else to do, I would have been bored without this occupation, which became an absorbing interest and kept me busy for hours. The time passed surprisingly fast. In some ways I was better off than I had been at home. It was exceedingly cold, but I was warm in my room, having organized a daily supply of logs for the stove. No fuel problem existed here, close to these great forests. To think of the ice coming nearer all the time was very disturbing. But for the present the harbor remained open, occasional ships came and went. From these I sometimes managed to obtain a few delicacies to supplement my meals at the café, which were ample, but lacking in variety. I had arranged for my food to be served in a sort of alcove off the main room, where I was out of the noise and smoke and had a certain amount of privacy.

The work I was supposed to be doing among the ruins enabled me to keep the High House unobtrusively under observation. I never once caught sight of the girl, although

on several occasions I saw the warden emerge, always
accompanied by his bodyguard. He usually jumped straight
into his big car and was driven off at tremendous speed. I
gathered that threats from political opponents accounted
for these precautions.

After two or three days I became impatient. I was getting
nowhere and time was short. As she never seemed to leave
the High House, I should have to get in. But no invitation
arrived. I was trying to decide on the best excuse for approaching the warden again when he sent one of his guards
to fetch me to lunch. The man intercepted me on my way to
the café at midday. I disliked the absence of notice, and the
whole imperious style of the summons and its delivery. It
was more a command than an invitation, and, feeling
obliged to protest, I said it was hardly possible to cancel the
meal already prepared and waiting for me at that very
moment. Instead of answering me, the guard shouted. Two
more black tunics appeared from nowhere: the wearer of
one was sent to explain things to the café proprietor, while
the other stationed himself beside me. I now had no alterna-
tive but to go with this double escort. Of course I was glad
to do so, it was what I wanted. But I would have preferred
less high-handed treatment.

The warden led me straight into a large dining hall with
a long table intended for twenty people. He took his chair
at the head, an imposing figure. I was seated beside him. A
third place was laid opposite. Seeing me glance at it, he
said: "A young friend from your country is staying with me;
I thought you might like to meet her." He gave me one of his
piercing looks as I replied calmly that I would be delighted.
Inwardly I was exulting; it seemed almost too good to be
true, the climax of my good fortune, to be spared the tricky
business of asking to see her.

Dry Martinis were brought in a frosted jug. Immediately
afterward someone came in, whispered something, gave
him a note. His face changed as he read the few words, he
ripped the paper across and across, reducing it to minute

fragments. "It appears the young person is indisposed." I hid my disappointment by murmuring something polite. He was frowning furiously, obviously could not bear to be thwarted over the least thing; his anger pervaded the atmosphere. Saying no more to me, he signed for the extra setting to be removed, glasses and cutlery were whipped out of sight. The food was served, but he hardly touched what was on his plate, sat pounding the shreds of paper into a pulp with his clenched fist. I became more and more annoyed the longer he ignored me, particularly resenting this additional rudeness after the peremptory way he had sent for me. I wanted to get up and walk out, but knew it would be fatal to break off relations at this stage. To distract myself, I thought of the girl, decided I was probably responsible for her absence; she must have guessed who I was, if she had not known all along. I tried to imagine her alone in a silent room overhead. But she seemed miles away, a dream figure, inaccessible and unreal.

The warden gradually became calmer, although his expression remained forbidding. I would not speak first, but waited for him to acknowledge my presence. A joint of excellent young lamb was carved, and while we were eating he referred abruptly to my investigations. "I notice you confine them to the ruins in my vicinity." I was disconcerted, I had not known I was being watched. Luckily there was a ready-made answer. "As you know, these have always been the administrative buildings, so anything of interest is more likely to turn up here than anywhere else." He said nothing, but made the sound of a player whose opponent claims a dubious point in the game. I could not tell whether my reply had satisfied him or not.

Coffee was put on the table, and to my surprise, everybody withdrew from the room. I felt apprehensive, I could not imagine what he could have to say to me in private. His mood appeared to have hardened; he looked formidable, cold, distant. It was difficult to believe he had ever showed friendliness when he remarked ominously: "People who try

to trick me usually regret it; I'm not easily taken in." His
voice was controlled and quiet, but the threat I had detected
in it on a former occasion had become open. I said I did not
understand what he meant; the obvious implication did not
apply to me. He subjected me to a prolonged stare, which I
returned with more coolness than I was feeling. An aura of
danger and duplicity surrounded him, I was on my guard.

Pushing aside his cup, he leaned his elbows on the table,
brought his face close to mine and went on gazing fixedly at
me without a word. His eyes were startlingly bright, I could
feel them trying to dominate me, and found it hard not to
lower my own. He must have practiced hypnosis at some
time: I had to keep up a sustained effort of resistance. It was
a relief when he drew back a little, and said bluntly: "I want
you to do something for me." "What on earth can I possibly do for you?" I was astonished. "Listen. This is a small,
poor, backward country, without resources. In an emergency we would be lost without the help of the big powers.
Unfortunately the big powers consider us too insignificant
to be of any interest. I want you to convince your government that we can be useful, if only because of our geo-
graphical position. I'm assuming you have the necessary
influence?" I supposed I had; but I was taken back, I had
not expected anything like this. My instinct was against it,
and I began: "That sort of thing's not my line at all—" He
interrupted impatiently: "I'm simply asking you to point
out to your politicians the advantage of co-operating with
us. It should be easy. They've only got to look at the map."
Before I could think what to say, he pressed me again with
increased impatience: "Well, will you do it?" His habit of
dominance and his personal magnetism made it virtually
impossible to refuse; almost involuntarily, I made a sound
of assent. "Good. It's a bargain. Of course you'll receive an
adequate return." As if to clinch the matter, he stood up
and held out his hand, adding: "You'd better write immediately to prepare the ground." He picked up a small silver
bell, rang it vigorously, people came trooping into the room.

As he went to meet them, he dismissed me with a casual nod. I felt confused and uneasy, and was glad to get out of the place. I did not like this new turn of events, I had the impression my luck was changing.

A day or two later his big car stopped beside me and he looked out, wearing a magnificent fur-lined overcoat. He wanted a word with me; would I come to the High House? I got in, we raced up to the entrance.

We went into a room full of people waiting to speak to him: the guards moved them back so that we could pass through to a room beyond. I heard him mutter, "Get rid of this fellow after five minutes," before he dismissed his men. To me he said: "I presume you've written to someone about that bargain of ours?" I muttered something evasive. In quite a different tone he rapped out: "The post office informs me you have not communicated with any useful person. I took you for a man of your word; it seems I was mistaken." To avoid a quarrel I took no notice of the insult, replied peaceably: "I haven't heard yet what I'm to get out of the bargain." Curtly he told me to state my terms. I decided to speak in a frank, simple manner, hoping to make him less hostile. "My request seems almost too trivial to mention after these preliminaries." I gave him what I hoped was a disarming smile. "It's simply this: I believe your guest may be an old acquaintance of mine, and should like to meet her in order to settle the point." I was careful not to show too much interest.

He said nothing, but I could feel opposition behind his silence. Evidently there had been a change in his attitude since the day when he had proposed to introduce us at lunch. Now I felt pretty sure he would not agree to the meeting.

Suddenly remembering the time, I looked at my watch. The five minutes had almost gone. I had no intention of waiting until the guards came in, according to orders, to throw me out, and began to make the opening moves of departure. He came to the door with me, kept his hand on the knob, preventing me from leaving. "She's been unwell, and is nervous about meeting people. I shall have to ask if she'll see you." I was convinced he would not allow the meeting to take place, and looked at my watch again. There was only one minute left. "I really must go now. I've taken up too much of your time already." His unexpected laughter took me by surprise; he must have known what was going on in my head. His mood seemed to alter suddenly, all at once his manner was easy. Once more I was momentarily aware of an obscure sense of inner contact with him. He opened the door and gave an order to the men standing out-side, who saluted and marched away down the corridor, their boots thumping on the polished floor. He turned to me then, and as if demonstrating his goodwill, said: "We can go to her now, if you like. But I'll have to prepare her first."

He took me back into the crowded waiting-room, where everybody surged round, eager to speak to him. He had a smile and a friendly word for those nearest, raised his voice to apologize generally for keeping them waiting, begged them all to be patient a few minutes longer, promised that everyone would be heard in due course. In a tone audible all over the room, he demanded: "Why is there no music?" then spoke sharply to a subordinate. "You know these peo-ple are my guests. The least we can do is try to entertain them if they have to wait." The notes of a string quartet started to fill the room, and followed us out of it.

He led the way past more guards, strode quickly along winding corridors ahead of me, ran up and down several flights of stairs. It was all I could do to keep pace with him. He was in far better condition that I was, and seemed to enjoy demonstrating the fact, looking back at me, laughing, showing off his fine physique. I did not quite trust this sud-den good humor. But I admired his tough athlete's body, the wide shoulders and elegant, narrow waist. The passages seemed never-ending. I was breathless, he had to wait for me finally, standing at the top of yet another short staircase. The landing was in deep shadow, I could just distinguish the rectangle of a single door, and realized that the stairs led only to this one room.

He told me to stay where I was for a minute while he explained the situation to the girl, adding, with a malicious grin: "It'll give you time to cool off a bit." With his hand on the door knob, he went on: "You understand, don't you, that it's entirely up to her to decide. There's nothing I can do if she prefers not to see you." He opened the door without knocking and vanished into the room.

Left out there in the semi-darkness, I felt gloomy and irritated. He seemed to have got the better of me by a trick. Nothing satisfactory to myself could come of an interview arranged and introduced by him. Most probably it would not materialize at all; either she would refuse to see me, or he would forbid her to do so. In any case, I did not want to talk to her in his presence, when she would be under his influence.

I listened, but could hear nothing through the soundproofed wall. After some moments I went down the stairs and wandered round dark passages until I met a servant who showed me the way out. My lucky period certainly seemed to be over.

FIVE

My window overlooked an empty landscape where nothing ever moved. No houses were visible, only the debris of the collapsed wall, a bleak stretch of snow, the fjord, the fir forest, the mountains. No color, only monotonous shades of gray from black to the ultimate dead white of the snow. The water lifeless in its dead calm, the ranks of black trees marching everywhere in uniform gloom. Suddenly there was a movement, a shout of red and blue in that silent gray monotone. I seized my overcoat, struggled into it as I rushed to the door; changed my mind and went back to the window, which was stuck fast. I managed to heave it up, stepped out on to piles of rubble, then pulled it shut behind me with the tips of my fingers. Slithering on the frozen grass, I ran down the slope; it was the quickest way; and I had eluded the woman of the house, whom I suspected of keeping watch on my movements. There was no one on the narrow path skirting the fjord, but the person I was chasing could not be far off. The path plunged into the forest. At once it got colder and darker under the trees, which grew close together, their black branches meeting in dense entanglements overhead, intertwining with the undergrowth lower down. Twenty invisible people could have been near me, but I saw the ghostly gray coat flicker among the firs, and occasionally caught a glimpse of its checked lining. The wearer's head was uncovered: her bright hair shimmered like silver fire, an *ignis fatuus* glimmering in the forest. She hurried on as fast as she could, anxious to get out of the trees. She was nervous in the forest, which always seemed full of menace. The crowding trees unnerved her, transformed themselves into black walls, shutting her in. It was late, after sunset; she had come too far and must hurry back. She looked about for the fjord, failed to see it, lost her bearings, and at once became really frightened, terrified of being overtaken by night in the dark forest. Fear was the climate she lived in; if she had ever known kindness it would have been different. The trees seemed to obstruct her with deliberate malice. All her life she had thought of herself as a foredoomed victim, and now the forest had become the malign force that would destroy her. In desperation she tried to run, but a hidden root tripped her, she almost fell. Branches caught in her hair, tugged her back, lashed out viciously when they were disentangled. The silver hairs torn from her head glittered among black needles; they were the clues her pursuers would follow, leading them to their victim. She escaped from the forest at length only to see the fjord waiting for her. An evil effluence rose from the water, something primitive, savage, demanding victims, hungry for a human victim.

For a second she stood still, appalled by the absolute silence and loneliness all around. A new ferocity pervaded the landscape now that night was approaching. She saw the massed armies of forest trees encamped on all sides, the mountain wall above bristling with trees like guns. Below, the fjord was an impossible icy volcano erupting the baleful fire of the swallowed sun.

In the deepening dusk every horror could be expected. She was afraid to look, tried not to see the spectral shapes rising from the water, but felt them come gliding toward her and fled in panic. One overtook her, wound her in soft, clammy, adhesive bands like ectoplasm. Wildly choking a scream, she fought herself free, raced on blindly, frantic and gasping. Her brain was locked in nightmare, she did not think. The last light fading, she stumbled against unseen rocks, bruising knees and elbows. Thorns lacerated her hands, scratched her face. Her flying leaps shattered the thin ice at the fjord's edge and she was deluged in freezing water. Each breath was painful, a sharp knife repeatedly stabbing her chest. She dared not stop or slacken speed for an instant, terrified by the loud thud of pursuing steps close behind her, not recognizing her own agonized heartbeats. Suddenly she slipped on the edge of a snowdrift, could not stop herself, fell face down in a deep snow-grave. There was snow in her mouth, she was done for, finished, she would never get up again, could not run any further. Cruelly straining muscles relentlessly forced her up, she had to struggle on, pulled by the irresistible magnet of doom. Systematic bullying when she was most vulnerable had distorted the structure of her personality, made a victim of her, to be destroyed, either by things or by human beings, people or fjords and forests; it made no difference, in any case she could not escape. The irreparable damage inflicted had long ago rendered her fate inevitable.

A pitch black mass of rock loomed ahead, a hill, a mountain, an unlighted fortress, buttressed by regiments of black firs. Her weak hands were shaking too much to manipulate a door, but the waiting forces of doom dragged her inside.

Stretched out on her bed, she could feel the hostile, alien, freezing dark pressed to the wall like the ear of a listening enemy. In the utter silence and solitude, she lay watching the mirror, waiting for her fate to arrive. It would not be long now. She knew that something fearful was going to happen in the soundproof room, where nobody could or would come to her rescue. The room was antagonistic as it always had been. She was aware of the walls refusing protection, of the frigid hostility in the air. There was nothing she could do, no one to whom she could appeal. Abandoned, helpless, she could only wait for the end.

A woman came in without knocking and stood in the doorway, handsome, forbidding, dressed all in black, tall and menacing as a tree, followed by other indistinct shapes, which kept to the shadows behind her. The girl at once recognized her executioner, whose enmity she had always felt without understanding it, too innocent or too preoccupied with her own dream world to guess the obvious cause. Now, cold bright pitiless eyes swam in the glassy depths of the mirror, darted toward their victim. *Her* eyes were widely dilated and black with dread, two deep pits of terror, of intuitive nightmare foreknowledge. Then a sense of fatality overcame her; she experienced a regression, became a submissive, terrorized child, cowed by persistent ill-treatment. Intimidated, obedient to the woman's commanding voice, she got up and with faltering steps left the platform, her white face blank as paper. When her arms were seized she cried out, struggled feebly. A hand was clamped over her mouth. Several figures towered above her. She was gripped from all sides, roughly handled, hustled out of the room, her hands tied behind her back.

Under the trees it got darker and darker, I kept losing sight of the path. In the end I lost it entirely and came out at a different place. I was close to the wall. It was impressive, intact, no break in it anywhere; I saw the black shapes of sentries posted along the top. Two of them were approaching each other and would cross quite near me. I stood still in the shadow of the black trees where I should not be seen. Their steps were loud, the hard frost magnified every sound. They met, stamped their feet, exchanged passwords, separated again. I walked on when the footsteps grew fainter. I had a curious feeling that I was living on several planes simultaneously; the overlapping of these planes was confusing. Huge rounded boulders as big as houses, resembling the heads of decapitated giants, were lying near, where they had fallen long ago from the mountainside. Suddenly I heard voices, looked everywhere, but could see no one. The sound seemed to come from among the boulders, so I went to investigate. A light flowered yellow in the blue dusk: I was looking at a cottage, not a mass of rock. People were talking inside it.

I heard yells, crashes, the frightened neighing of horses,

all the noises of battle. Arrows flew in clouds. War clubs thumped. There was loud clashing of steel. Strangely dressed men came at the wall in waves, swarming up it, using their feet as well as their hands, holding cutlasses in their teeth. Agile as gorillas, they came in their thousands; however many were thrown back, a new wave always came on. Finally all the defenders of the wall were exterminated, the second line defenses forced back. Invaders already inside opened the gates, and the rest burst in like a tidal wave. People barricaded themselves in their houses. In the town there was utter chaos. Hand-to-hand fighting in the narrow streets; savage meaningless cries like the cries of wild animals resounding between the walls. The strangers raced through the town like madmen, pouring wine down their throats, slaughtering all they met, every man, woman, child, animal. The wine streamed down their faces mingled with sweat and blood so that they looked like demons. A little snow fell: this seemed to excite them to frenzy, they laughed insanely, tried to catch the falling flakes in their mouths. The horsemen carried long lances with pennants or feathers attached. Hacked-off heads were impaled on these lances, sometimes infants or dogs. Huge fires blazed everywhere, it was as bright as day. The air was full of the reek of burning, of charred wood and old dust. As people were smoked out of their homes they were massacred by the enemy. Many preferred to die in the flames.

I had no weapon, and searched for something with which to defend myself. I was in a street where dead horses had been piled up to form a barricade, among them a man who had been killed with his mount. He had not had time even to draw his sword, which was still in the scabbard, engraved with intricate patterns, a beautiful piece of work. I tugged at the projecting hilt, but in falling the blade had jammed and I could not move it. The dead beasts had been heaped up in such frantic haste that my persistent efforts were shaking the whole construction; carcasses worked loose, rolled down, forming a breech. Before I could repair the damage, a troop

of horsemen galloped along the street with a fearful clattering din, waving their lances, yelling their senseless cries. I
threw myself flat on the ground, hoping they had not seen
me, expecting the worst. As they came up, one of them
jabbed his long lance ahead of him into the dead rider, dislodging the body so violently that it fell on top of me, probably saving my life. I kept perfectly still while the whole
troop went careering past, rolling their bloodshot, demented,
animalic eyes.

When they had gone, I pushed the corpse aside and got
up to go and search for the girl. I had not much hope of
finding her; I knew the fate of girls in sacked towns. The
sword was loose now, I pulled it out easily. I had never used
such a weapon and tried slashing at some of the bodies I
passed. The thing was heavy and hard to handle, but I discovered the balance and began to get the feel of it as I
walked, thus gaining some much-needed confidence. As it
happened, I was not attacked. Most of the fighting was
going on in the lower streets, round the harbor forts, which
appeared to be holding out. When I saw anyone I took
cover, and in the general confusion escaped observation.
The High House was almost burned out already, only the
shell still standing. Smoke and flames spouted toward the
sky, the whole interior was incandescent. I approached as
close as I could, but was driven back by the smoke and the
intense heat. It was quite impossible to get inside. In any
case, nobody could have survived in such an inferno. My
face was scorched, sparks were smoldering in my hair, I
crushed them out with my hands.

I came upon her by chance, not far away, lying face down
on the stones. A little blood had trickled out of her mouth.
Her neck had an unnatural twist; a living girl could not
have turned her head at that angle: the neck was broken.
She had been dragged by the hair, hands which had twisted
it into a sort of rope had dulled its silvery brightness. On
her back blood was still fresh in places, wet and bright red;
in other places it had caked black on the white flesh. I

looked particularly at one arm, on which the circular marks of teeth stood out clearly. The bones of the forearm were broken, the sharp pointed ends of bone projected at the wrist through the torn tissue. I felt I had been defrauded: I alone should have done the breaking with tender love; I was the only person entitled to inflict wounds. I leaned forward and touched her cold skin.

I went to look in at the cottage window, taking care not to go near enough to be seen from inside. A lot of people were crowded into a small smoky room, firelight flickering red on their faces, reminding me of a medieval picture of hell. At first I could not make out any words; they were all talking at once. I recognized one woman, unusually tall, handsome in a forbidding way; I had seen her at the High House. Now she was with a man she called father who sat just inside the window. Because he was so close to me, his was the first voice I understood. He was relating the legend of the fjord, how every year at the winter solstice a beautiful girl had to be sacrificed to the dragon that lived in its depths. The other voices gradually became silent when he began describing the rite itself. "We untie her as soon as we get her up there on the rock. She must struggle a bit, otherwise the dragon might think we'd palmed off a dead girl on him. The water foams down below. The monster's great scaly coils appear. Then we hurl her down. The whole fjord becomes a maelstrom, blood and foam flying in all directions."

A lively discussion of the sacrifice followed, different people speaking in turn. They might have been talking about a football match between their team and a rival town. Somebody said: "We haven't so many good-looking girls to spare. Why should we give one of them to the dragon? Why not sacrifice a stranger, some foreign girl who means nothing to any of us?" The tone of voice suggested that the speaker referred to a special person, whose identity was known to all present. The father started raising objections, but was silenced by his daughter, who called out her agreement, launching into a vicious tirade of which I only caught isolated phrases. "Pale girls who look as pure as if they were made of glass . . . smash them to smithereens . . . And I *will* smash this one . . ." The end was shouted. "I'll hurl her down off the rock myself, if none of you have the guts to do it!"

I walked away in disgust. These people were worse than savages. My hands and face were numb, I felt half frozen, and could not think why I had stood there so long listening to their preposterous rigmarole. I had a vague feeling that something was wrong with me, although I could not decide what it was. For a moment this was disturbing; then I forgot it. A small, cold, bright moon shone high in the sky, showed the landscape distinctly. I recognized the fjord but not the scene. Tall perpendicular rocks rose straight out of the water, supporting a flat horizontal rock like a high-diving platform. Some people appeared, dragging the girl between them, her hands tied. As she passed me, I caught a glimpse of her pitiful white face of a child-victim, terrified and betrayed. I sprang forward, tried to reach her, to cut her bonds. Somebody went for me. I threw him off, tried again to get near her, she was dragged away. I rushed after the group, shouting: "Murderers!" Before I could overtake them, they were hauling her up the rock.

I was close to her on the platform high above the fjord. We were alone there, although a mixture of vague sounds behind me indicated the presence of numerous onlookers. They did not concern me. I was completely concentrated on the trembling figure, half kneeling, half crouching, at the extremity of the rock, overhanging the dark water. Her hair glittered as if with diamond dust under the moon. She was not looking at me, but I could see her face, which was always pale, but now drained of color right to the bone. I observed her extreme slenderness, felt I could enclose the whole of her with my two hands, even the rib-cage containing her heart. Her skin was like white satin, shadowless in the brilliant moonlight. The circular marks the cords had left on her wrists would have been red in daylight, but now looked black. I could imagine how it would feel to take hold of her wrists and to snap the fragile bones with my hands.

Leaning forward, I touched her cold skin, the shallow hollow in her thigh. Snow had fallen between her breasts.

Armed men came up, pushed me back, seized her by her frail shoulders. Big tears fell from her eyes like icicles, like diamonds, but I was unmoved. They did not seem to me like real tears. She herself did not seem quite real. She was pale and almost transparent, the victim I used for my own enjoyment in dreams. People behind me muttered, impatient at the delay. The men did not wait any longer but hurled her down, her last pathetic scream trailing after her. The night exploded then like a paper bag. Huge jets of water sprang up; waves dashing wildly against the rocks burst in cascades of spray. I hardly noticed the freezing showerbath, but peered over the edge of the platform, and saw a circle of scaly coils emerge from the seething water, in which something white struggled frantically for an instant before the crunch of armor-plated jaws.

I was in a hurry to get back to my lodging. My feet and fingers were numb, my face stiff, my head starting to ache with the cold. As soon as I had thawed out a little in my warm room, I began to write. My main topic, of course, was the Indris, but I still kept up the pretense I had started by writing down anything that seemed of interest about the town. I did not think the security people would bother to read my notes, although they could easily do so while I was out of the room. The childishly simple form of scrambling I used, mixing up sentences about the lemurs with others on local affairs, would at least defeat the woman of the house, who pried into everything.

I derived great satisfaction from describing the gentle mysterious singing creatures, and seemed to grow more deeply involved with them as I wrote. With their enchanting other-world voices, their gay, affectionate, innocent ways, they had become for me symbols of life as it could be on earth, if man's destructiveness, violence and cruelty were eliminated. I enjoyed writing as a rule, the sentences came to me without effort, as if they formed in my head of their own accord. But now it was quite different, I could not find the right words: I knew I was not expressing myself lucidly, or remembering accurately, and after some minutes put down my pen. Immediately I saw a mental picture of many people crowded into a smoky room, and felt I ought to inform the warden of what I had overheard. At the same time, there was a curious unreality about the memory of that scene, as if I could have dreamt it. And when it occurred to me that the girl might be in real danger I did not quite believe this. I got up, all the same, to go to the telephone. Then, restrained by the peculiar uncertainty as to what was real more than the thought of the woman who would be listening to every word, I decided not to ring up until I got to the café.

My sense of unreality became overwhelming as I left the house. A strong colorless light was making everything outside as clear as day, although I was quite unable to see where it came from. My amazement increased when I observed that this extraordinary light revealed details not normally visible to the naked eye. It was snowing slightly, and the complex structure of each individual snowflake appeared in crystalline clearness, the delicate star-like, flower-like forms perfectly distinct and as bright as jewels. I looked round for the familiar ruins, but they were no longer there. I was used to the sight of destruction, but this was different. Nothing whatever was left of the ruined town; its structures had disintegrated, the remains were flattened, spread as though a giant steam-roller had passed over them. The one or two vertical fragments seemed to have been left intentionally, with the deliberate object of emphasizing the general leveling. With a dreamlike feeling, I walked on, seeing no one, either alive or dead. The air was full of a sweetish smell, not unpleasant, which I could smell on my own hands and clothes, and presumed had been left by some gas. The absence of fires surprised me; nothing seemed to be burning, I saw no smoke. I only now noticed thin trickles of a white milky fluid moving among the debris, collecting in pools here and there. These white pools continually widened as the liquid eroded their edges, eating away whatever came in contact with it; it was only a question of time before the entire mass of wreckage would be disposed of in this way. I stood still for a moment to watch the process, fascinated by such a practical, thorough method of clearance. I remembered that I had to find the girl, searched for her desperately through the endless rubble. I thought I saw her a long way off in the distance, shouted, ran; she changed, disappeared. Like a mirage I saw her still further away; then she vanished again. A girl's arm protruded from a heap of detritus; I took hold of the wrist, pulled gently; it came away in my hand. All at once I heard sounds and movements behind me, quickly swung round, caught sight of living objects which moved with a gliding motion, made warbling noises. Their shapes were queer, only partially human, reminding me of mutants in science fiction stories. They took no notice of me, ignored my existence completely, and I hurried on without going any closer.

When I came to a place where bodies were lying about, I stopped to examine them in case one was hers. I went up to the nearest corpse and looked at it carefully. It was not recognizable, the skeleton and what was left of the flesh had become phosphorescent. To look at the others would only be wasting time, so I left them alone.

SIX

The owner of the house heard me pass her door, opened it, peered out frowning. I pretended not to have seen her and hurried on, but the outer door would not move, there was some obstruction. I pushed hard, scattering the snow piled against it, and letting in icy wind that rattled something behind me. There was an angry shout, "Mind what you're doing!" which I ignored.

Outside I was astonished by the quantity of snow that had fallen. A different town, white and spectral, had replaced the old one. The few feeble lights showed how the shapes of the ruins were altered by their thick white covering, the details of destruction obscured, all outlines muffled and blurred. The effect of the heavy snowfall was to deprive structures of solidity and precise location: my old impression revived of a scene made of nylon with nothing behind. Only a few snowflakes were in the air at first; then a white flurry passed me, driven along parallel to the ground by the strong wind. I lowered my head against this freezing wind, and saw the small grains of snow, dry and frozen, swirling round my legs. The flurries thickened, became incessant, filling the air; I could not see where I was. I got only intermittent glimpses of my surroundings, which seemed vaguely familiar, and yet distorted, unreal. My ideas were confused. In a peculiar way, the unreality of the outer world appeared to be an extension of my own disturbed state of mind.

Collecting my thoughts with an effort, I remembered that the girl was in danger and must be warned. I gave up trying to find the café, and decided to go straight to the warden. I could just make out the fort-like mass of his home looming over the town.

Except for the main square, the streets were always deserted after dark, so I was amazed to see quite a number of figures climbing the steep hill in front of me. Next moment I remembered hearing talk, without paying attention, of some public dinner or celebration at the High House, which evidently was being held tonight. I reached the entrance only a few steps behind the nearest group of people, and was glad they were there; without them, I should not have been sure this was the right place, the snow made everything look so different. Two hillocks, one on each side, might have been the batteries; but there were other white mounds I could not account for. A cluster of long pointed icicles, sharp as swords, clung to a lantern over the huge main door, glistening ferociously in the dim light. As those ahead of me were admitted, I stepped forward and went inside with them. The guards would most likely have let me in if I had been alone, but this seemed the easiest way.

Nobody took the least notice of me. I must have been recognized, but received no sign of recognition from anyone, felt increasingly derealized, as familiar faces came up and passed me without a glance. The gloomy great place was already crowded, the group I had come in with must have been one of the last. If this was a celebration, it was singularly subdued. All the faces were dour as usual; there was no laughing and little talking. Such conversation as went on took place in tones too low to be overheard.

Ceasing to notice the people, I considered how I was to reach the girl. The warden had taken me to the door of her room, but I knew I would never be able to find it again without a guide. Somebody would have to help me. Wondering who would be the best person to approach, I wandered from room to room, presently found myself in a huge vaulted hall, where trestle tables had been set up, with jugs and bottles of wine and spirits placed at intervals between vast platters of meat and bread. Standing in a dark corner where I would not be seen, I watched the servants bringing in more plates of food and arranging them on the tables. In spite of an almost feverish anxiety over the girl, instead of attempting to find her I stood there doing nothing at all; became aware of an odd sort of fragmentation of my ideas.

Hundreds of torches flared, lighting the great hall, a banquet had been arranged to celebrate victory. I went first with one of my aides to look over the prisoners. It was the commander's traditional privilege, a routine. The women were herded together behind a barrier. They had already retreated as far from everyone as they could, but when they saw us coming contrived to move back further still, pressing against the wall. They did not attract me. I could not tell one from another; suffering had given them all the same features. In other parts of the hall there was much noise, but here only silence; no pleadings, no curses, no lamentations; just staring eyes, the red flicker of torchlight on naked limbs, breasts.

Torches were fixed like bundles of rockets to the enormous pillars supporting the high arched roof. Leaning against one of these pillars a young girl stood a little apart, unclothed except by her shining hair. The death of hope had tranquilized her white face. She was scarcely more than a child, did not see us; her eyes were looking far inward at dreams. Arms like peeled wands, silvery streaming hair . . . a young moon among clouds . . . I wanted to stay and watch her. But they came to escort me to the presence.

His splendid gold seat was carved with the faces and exploits of heroes, his ancestors. His magnificent cloak, lined with sable and gold-embroidered, draped his knees in stiff statuesque folds. Sparks dripped from the torches and warmed the cold white of his long, thin, restless hands. A blue flash from his eyes: a matching blue flash from a tremendous jewel worn on his hand. I did not know the name of this stone. Neither his hands nor his eyes were ever at rest, there was a constant bombardment of blue. He would not let me move to a different place, kept me standing beside him. Because I had led the victorious army, he gave me a glittering order I did not want: I had too many already. I told him I only wanted the girl. A gasp went up. The people round him waited to see me struck down. I was indifferent. I had lived half my life, seen as much as I wanted. I was sick of war, sick of serving this difficult, dangerous master who loved war and killing and nothing else. There was a kind of insanity in his war-making. Conquest was not enough. He wanted a war of extermination, all enemies slaughtered without exception, nobody left alive. He wanted to kill me. But, although he could not live without war, he was unable to plan a campaign, take a city; I had to do that. So he could not kill me. He wanted my war skills and he wanted me dead. Now he gave me a deadly glance, kept me at his side; but, at the same time, beckoned closer those standing round him. They formed a close sycophantic circle, the only gap was the point where I stood. A small man slipped in, crept under my arm, lifted a long-nosed face like a vicious dog ready to bite, cringing before his master, snarling at me. Now the circle was closed. But I could still watch the ring flashing blue, the gesticulations of the unquiet hands, their long thin white fingers and long pointed nails. The fingers curved inwards in a strange way, like a strangler's, the blue stone was anchored by the curved bone. Commands were given, too low for me to hear. Earlier, he had praised my skill and courage extravagantly, promised me great rewards, I was his guest of honor. I knew him well, could well imagine what sort of reward he planned for me now. I had already prepared my face.

Six guards brought her to him, bundled up in a soldier's cloak. These men had been taught a trick of grasping that left no bruises. I had never learned it, did not see now how it was done. There was a moment's pause. I wondered if, after all, generosity might be shown . . . in the circumstances, it seemed just possible.

Then I saw his hand move toward her, the curved predatory fingers, the blazing blue. She gave a small choked cry as the huge ring tore through her hair: it was the one time I heard her voice. I heard too the faint clank of the metal rings round her wrists and ankles when she fell with violence across his knees. I stood motionless, looking on with an expressionless face. That cold, hard, mad, murderous man; her soft young girl's body and dreaming eyes . . . a pity, sad . . .

I had decided to approach one of the servants who were still busy round the long tables. I was watching a scared-looking peasant girl, one of the youngest of them, slow, clumsy and obviously new to the work. She seemed frightened, downtrodden, the others teased her, slapped her, jeered, called her half-witted. She was tearful, kept making mistakes, I saw her drop things several times. Her sight could have been defective. I went and stood in a doorway she had to pass, grabbed her and dragged her through, my hand over her mouth. Luckily, the passage beyond was empty. While I was saying I would not harm her, only wanted her help, she looked at me in horror, her red eyes filling with tears; blinked, trembled, seemed too stupid to understand. There was no time, in a moment people would come looking for her, but she would not speak. I spoke to her kindly; argued with her; shook her; showed her a wad of notes. Absolutely no response, no reaction. Increasing the amount of money, I held it under her nose, told her: "Here's your chance to get away from people who treat you badly. With this you won't have to work again for a long time." Finally she saw the point, agreed to take me to the room.

We started off, but she was slow and kept hesitating, so that I began to wonder whether she really knew the way. My nerves were on edge, I wanted to hit her, it was hard to control myself. I was afraid of being too late. I said I had to speak to the warden, which would be impossible once the party had started. It was a relief to hear that he never appeared during the early part of the evening, but only when the eating and drinking were over, in about two hours' time. At last I recognized the final steep staircase. She pointed to the top, clutched the money I was holding ready for her, bolted back the way we had come.

I went up and opened the solitary door. The soundproof room was in darkness, but a little of the faint light from the landing came in behind me. I saw the girl lying on the bed, fully dressed, with a book beside her; she had fallen asleep while reading. I spoke her name softly. She started up, her hair glinting. "Who's that?" There was fear in her voice. I moved, let the dim light touch my face; she knew me at once, said: "What are you doing here?" I said: "You're in danger; I've come to take you away." "Why should I go with you?" She sounded astonished. "There's no difference—" We both heard a sound at the same moment; footsteps were starting to mount the stairs. I stepped back, froze, held my breath. The feeble light outside the door was extinguished. I stood in black shadow, I was pretty safe; unless she gave me away.

The man's ungentle hands gripped her. "Put on your outdoor things quickly. We're leaving at once." His voice was low and peremptory. "Leaving?" She stared, saw him as a blacker shadow against the black, her cold lips murmuring: "Why?" "Don't talk. Do as I tell you." Obediently she stood up, the draught from the door made her shiver. "How am I supposed to find anything in the dark? Can't we have a light?" "No. Somebody might see." He flashed a torch briefly, saw her pick up a comb and start pulling it through her hair, snatched it away from her. "Leave that! Get your coat on— hurry!" The irritable impatience radiating from him made her movements slower, more awkward. Feeling about the dark room, she found her coat but could not find the way into it; she held it the wrong way round. He seized it angrily, turned it, forced her arms through the sleeves. "And now come on! Don't make a sound. Nobody must know we've gone." "Where are we going? Why do we have to go at this time of night?" She expected no answer, doubted whether she heard correctly when he muttered, "It's the one chance," adding something about the approaching ice. He grasped her arm then, pulled her across the landing and on to the stairs. The beam of the torch, intermittently stabbing pitch blackness, showed his looming repressive shadow, which she followed as if sleepwalking through all the ramifications of the huge building, out into the icy snow-filled night.

Although snow was falling heavily, there was none on the black car; it had just been cleared away: yet no one had passed them, nobody was in sight. She shivered as she got in, sat in silence while he quickly inspected the chains. Yellow oblongs stained the pure white in front of the windows. In the air, the snow was transformed into showering gold as it passed the lights. A confused noise from the dining hall, voices, clattering plates, drowned the noise of the car starting up, and impelled her to ask: "What about all those people who are expecting you? Aren't you going to see them?"

Already in a state of irritable nervous tension, he was exasperated by the question, lifted one hand from the wheel in a threatening gesture. "I told you not to talk!" His voice was frightening, his eyes flashed in the dark interior of the car. She moved fast to avoid the blow, but could not get out of reach, crouched down, shielding herself with her raised arm, made no sound when the glancing blow struck her shoulder and crushed her against the door; afterward huddled there in silence, shrinking away from his silent rage.

Snow-muffled silence outside; silence filling the car. He drove without lights, his eyes like cats' eyes, able to see through the snowy darkness. A ghost-car, invisible, silent, fled from the ruined town. The ancient snow-covered fortifications fell back and vanished in snow, the broken wall vanished behind. In front loomed the black living wall of the forest, ghostly whiteness fuming along its crest like spray blown back from the crest of a breaking wave. She waited for the black mass to come crashing down on them, but there was no crash, only the silence of snow and forest outside, and in the car, his silence, her apprehension. He never spoke, never looked at her, handled the powerful car recklessly on the rough frozen track, hurling it at speed over

all obstacles, as if by the force of his will. The violent lurch-
ing of the car threw her about; she was not heavy enough to
keep in her seat. Thrown against him, forced to touch his
coat, she winced away as though the material burned. He
seemed unaware. She felt forgotten, forsaken.

It was incomprehensible to her, this extraordinary flight
that went on and on. The forest went on for ever. The silence
went on and on. The snow stopped, but the cold went on
and even increased, as if some icy exudation from the black
trees congealed beneath them. Hour after hour passed before
a little reluctant daylight filtered down through the roof of
branches, revealing nothing but gloomy masses of firs, dead
and living trees tangled together, a dead bird often caught
in the branches, as if the tree had caught it deliberately. She
shuddered, identifying herself, as a victim, with the dead
bird. It was she who had been snared by nets of black
branches. Armies of trees surrounded her on all sides, marching to infinity in all directions. Snow flew past the window
again, waving white flags. She was the one who long ago had
surrendered. She understood nothing of what was happening. The car leaped in the air, she was flung painfully on to
her bruised shoulder, tried ineffectually to shield it with the
other hand.

The man drove the car brutally throughout the short day.
It seemed to her that she had never known anything but this
terrifying drive in the feeble half-light; the silence, the cold,
the snow, the arrogant figure beside her. His cold statue's
eyes were the eyes of a Mercury, ice-eyes, mesmeric and menacing. She wished for hatred. It would have been easier. The
trees receded a little, a little more sky appeared, bringing the
last gleams of the fading light. Suddenly, she was astonished
to see two log huts, a gate between, blocking the road. Unless
the gate was opened they could not pass. She watched it racing toward them, reinforced with barbed wire and metal.
The car burst through with a tremendous shattering smash, a
great rending and tearing, a frantic metallic screeching. Broken glass showered her, she ducked instinctively as a long,

sharp, pointed sliver sliced the air just over her head, and the car rocked sickeningly on two wheels before turning over. At the last moment then, by some miracle of skill, or strength, or sheer willpower, the driver brought it back on to its axis again, and drove on as if nothing had happened.

Shouts exploded behind them. A few shots popped ineffectively and fell short. She glanced back and saw uniforms running; then the small commotion was over, cut off by black trees. The road improved on this side of the frontier, the car traveled faster, more smoothly. She shifted her position, leaning away from the stream of ice-vapor entering through the smashed window, shook bits of broken glass off her lap. There was blood on her wrists, both hands were cut and bleeding; she looked at them in remote surprise.

I raced down stairs and passages. In sight of the main door I hid in the shadows, watched the men guarding it. Sounds of the party, now growing more animated, came from the dining hall, where drinking was evidently in full swing. Someone shouted to the guards out in the cold corridor. The men I was watching put their heads together, then left their post, passed close to me as they went to join the rest. Unnoticed by anyone, I slipped out through the door they were supposed to be guarding.

It was snowing hard. I could barely distinguish the nearest ruins, white stationary shadows beyond the moving fabric of falling white. Snowflakes turned yellow like swarms of bees round the lighted windows. A wide expanse of snow lay in front of me, a hollow marking the place where the warden's black car had stood. I realized that various white mounds must be other cars, belonging, presumably, to his household, and waded toward them through the deep snow. I tried the door of the first one, found it unlocked. The whole vehicle was buried in snow, which had drifted deep against wheels and windscreen. Snow fell all over me when I opened the door, filled my sleeve as I tried to clean the glass. I thought the starter would never work, but at last the car began to move slowly forward. I revved the engine just

enough to keep the tires gripping, and followed the warden's hardly visible tracks, which were rapidly being obliterated by fresh snow. Outside the encircling wall they
practically vanished. I lost them altogether at the edge of
the forest, blindly drove into a tree, scraping off the bark.
The car stopped and refused to move. The wheels just spun
round, uselessly churning the snow. As I got out, a mass of
snow fell on me from the branches above. In two seconds
my clothes were caked solid with driving snow. I tore down
fir branches, threw them under the wheel, got back into the
car and restarted. It was no good; the tires would not grip,
still went on spinning and hissing. I was sliding sideways, I
pulled on the brake, jumped straight into a snowdrift, sank
up to my armpits. The snow kept collapsing on me as I
moved, slipped inside my collar, my shirt, I felt snow in my
navel; to struggle out was an exhausting business. After
breaking off more branches and piling them under the car
without the least effect, I knew I was beaten and would
have to give up. Weather conditions were quite impossible.
Somehow or other I got the car going, and crawled back to
the town. It was the only thing to do in the circumstances.

I started skidding again just as I reached the wall, lost control this time. Suddenly I saw the front wheels crumbling
the edge of a deep bomb-crater; one more second, and I would
be over; the drop was of many feet. I stood on the foot brake,
the car spun right round, executed a complete circle before I
jumped out and it nosedived, vanishing under the snow.

I was freezing, very tired, shivering so much I could
hardly walk. Luckily my lodging was not far off. I slithered
and staggered back there, crouched over the stove just as I
was, plastered in frozen snow, my teeth chattering. The
shivering was so violent I could not unfasten my coat, only
succeeded in dragging it off by slow stages. In the same
laborious fashion, by prolonged painful effort, I finally got
rid of the rest of my freezing clothes, struggled into a
dressing-gown. It was then that I saw the cable and ripped
open the envelope.

My informant reported the crisis due in the next few days. All air and sea services had ceased operating, but arrangements had been made to pick me up by helicopter in the morning. Still holding the flimsy paper, I crawled into bed, went on shivering under the piles of blankets. The warden must have received the news earlier in the day. He had fled to save himself, abandoning his people to their fate. Of course such conduct was highly reprehensible, scandalous: but I did not condemn him. I did not think I would have acted differently in his place. Nothing he could have done would have saved the country. If he had revealed the critical situation a panic would have resulted, the roads would have been jammed, nobody would have escaped. In any case, judging by what I had just experienced, his chance of reaching the frontier was extremely slim.

SEVEN

The aircraft deposited me at a distant port just before the ship sailed. I was suffering from some kind of fever, shivering, aching, apathetic. I sat at the back of the car rushing me to the docks, did not even look out, went on board in a daze. The ship was already moving when I crossed the deck, meaning to go straight to my cabin. But now the scene caught my eye, and it gave me a shock; I stopped and stood staring. A sunlit harbor was sliding past me, a busy town; I saw wide streets, well-dressed people, modern buildings, cars, yachts on the blue water. No snow; no ruins; no armed guards. It was a miracle, a flashback to something dreamed. Then another shock, the sensation of a violent awakening, as it dawned on me that this was the reality, and those other things the dream. All of a sudden the life I had lately been living appeared unreal: it simply was not credible any longer. I felt a huge relief, it was like emerging into sunshine from a long cold black tunnel. I wanted to forget what had just been happening, to forget the girl and the senseless, frustrating pursuit I had been engaged in, and think only about the future.

Later, when the fever left me, my feelings remained unchanged. Thankful to have escaped from the past, I decided to go to the Indris; to make that tropical island my home, and the lemurs themselves my life work. I would devote the rest of my time to studying them, writing their history, recording their strange songs. No one else had done it, as far as I knew. It seemed a satisfactory project, a worthwhile aim.

From the shop on board I bought a big notebook and a stock of ball-point pens. I was ready to plan my work. But I could not concentrate. After all, I had not escaped the past. My thoughts kept wandering back to the girl; incredible that I should have wished to forget her. Such a forgetting would have been monstrous, impossible. She was like a part of me, I could not live without her. But now I wanted to go to the Indris, so there was a conflict. She prevented me, holding me back with thin arms.

I tried to stop thinking about her, to fix my mind on those innocent gentle creatures, their sweet, eerie singing. But she persistently distracted me with thoughts that were less than innocent. Her face haunted me: the sweep of her long lashes, her timid enchanting smile; and then a change of expression I could produce at will, a sudden shift, a bruised look, a quick change to terror, to tears. The strength of the temptation alarmed me. The black descending arm of the executioner; my hands seizing her wrists . . . I was afraid the dream might turn out to be real . . . Something in her demanded victimization and terror, so she corrupted my dreams, led me into dark places I had no wish to explore. It was no longer clear to me which of us was the victim. Perhaps we were victims of one another.

I was desperately worried when I thought of the situation I had left behind. I walked round and round the decks, wondering what had happened, whether the warden had got away, whether she had been with him. No news was received on board ship. I could only wait, in great anxiety and impatience, to reach a port where I could go ashore and get some information. At last the day came. The steward had pressed my suit. He brought it back with a buttonhole, a red carnation he had got hold of somehow. Its strong color looked well against the light gray material.

Just as I was ready to leave my cabin, there was a peremptory bang on the door, and a plain-clothes policeman came in without waiting for me to answer. He did not take off his hat, but opened his jacket to show the official badge, the pistol in its armpit holster. I gave him my passport. He flipped over the pages contemptuously, looked me up and down in an insolent way, stared hard and with particular disapproval at the red carnation. Everything about my appearance obviously confirmed the low opinion he had already formed. I asked what he wanted with me, received no answer but an insulting silence: I would not ask again. He produced a pair of handcuffs, dangled them in front of me. I said nothing. When he tired of the jingling, he put them away, observing that, out of respect for my country, handcuffs would not be used. I was to be allowed to walk off the ship with him. But I had better not play any games.

The sun shone, everybody was going ashore. In the crowd I kept close beside him, as agreed. I was not worried. Such things happened. I gathered that I was wanted for interrogation, and wondered what questions I would be asked, and how they had got hold of my name. Uniformed police were waiting for us in a side street just off the quay. They ordered me into an armored car with black glass in the windows. After a short drive, we stopped at a large municipal building in a quiet square. Birds were singing. I noted the sound specially after the days at sea.

The few passers-by paid no attention to us. But a girl standing at the corner a few yards away took some interest, judging by her frequent glances in my direction. I saw that she was selling spring flowers, jonquils, dwarf irises, wild tulips, and among them a bunch of red carnations, like the one I was wearing. Then armed figures fell in round me, marched me into the building and down a long corridor. "Get a move on." A powerful hand gripped my elbow, pushed me up some steps. Double doors at the top opened into a hall where people sat in tiers as at a theater, a magistrate enthroned facing them. "In you go!" Various hard hands pulled and shoved me into a sort of pew. "Halt!" Feet stamped smartly to right and left, and I looked round, feeling detached from the situation. A high ceiling, closed windows, no sun, no singing birds, on each side of me men with guns, everywhere staring faces. People whispered or cleared their throats. The jury looked tired, or bored. Somebody read out my name and particulars, all quite correct. I confirmed them and took the oath.

The case was that a girl had vanished, supposed kidnapped, possibly murdered. A well-known person had been suspected and questioned, and had accused someone else who could not be found. The girl's name was mentioned; I was asked if I knew her. I replied that I had known her for several years. "You were intimate with her?" "We were old friends." There was laughter; somebody asked: "What was your relationship with her?" "I've told you; we were old friends." More laughter, silenced by an official. "You expect us to believe that you changed your plans all at once, dropped everything you were doing, in order to follow a friend to a foreign country?" They seemed to know all about me. I said: "That is the truth."

I sat on the bed, smoking, watching her face in the mirror as she combed her hair, the smooth sheen of the glittering mass of palely shining hair, its silvery fall on her shoulders. She leaned forward to look at herself, the glass reflected the beginning of her small breasts. I watched them move with her breathing, went and stood behind her, put my arms round her, covered them with my hands. She pulled away from me. Not wanting to see her frightened expression, I blew smoke in her face. She went on resisting, and I had an impulse to do certain things with the lighted cigarette, dropped it on the floor, put my foot on it. Then I pulled her closer to me. She struggled, cried: "Don't! Leave me alone! I hate you! You're cruel and treacherous . . . you betray people, break promises . . ." I was impatient, I let her go and went over to lock the door. Before I got there, a sound made me turn round. She was holding a big bottle of eau-de-Cologne over her head, meaning to hit me with it. I told her to put it down; she took no notice, so I went back and twisted it out of her hand. She was not strong enough to put up a fight. There was no more strength in her muscles than in a child's.

While she was getting dressed I continued to sit on the bed. We did not speak to each other. She was ready, fastening her coat, when the door opened suddenly: in my impatience just now, I had forgotten to go back and lock it. A man came in. I jumped up to throw him out, but he walked past as though I was invisible or not present.

A tall, athletic, arrogant-looking man, with an almost paranoid air of assurance. His very bright and blue eyes flashed a danger signal, seemed not to see me. The girl was petrified, she did nothing at all. I did nothing either, simply stood watching. It was unlike me. But he was a man who had entered with a revolver for a specific purpose, and could not be prevented from carrying it out. I wondered if he would shoot us both, and if so which first, or if only one of us, which one. Such points were of interest to me.

It was clear that he regarded her as his property. I considered that she belonged to me. Between the two of us she was reduced to nothing; her only function might have been to link us together. His face wore the look of extreme arrogance which always repelled me. Yet I suddenly felt an indescribable affinity with him, a sort of blood-contact, generating confusion, so that I began to wonder if there *were* two of us . . .

I was asked: "What happened when you met your friend?" "We did not meet." Subdued excitement broke out, an official voice had to order silence. The next voice sounded like an actor's, trained in elocution. "I wish to state that the witness is a psychopath, probably schizoid, and therefore not to be believed." Someone interjected: "Produce a psychiatrist's confirmation." The theatrical voice continued: "I repeat, with all possible emphasis, that this man is known to be a psychopath and totally unreliable. We are investigating an atrocious crime against an innocent pure young girl: I ask you to note his unnatural callousness, his indifferent expression. What cynicism to come here with that flower in his buttonhole! How arrogantly he displays his utter contempt for the sanctity of family life, and for all decent feeling! His attitude is not only abnormal, but depraved, infamous, a desecration of all we hold sacred . . ."

Somewhere high up in the room, where I could not see it, a bell rang. A superior, unimplicated voice stated: "A psychopath is not an acceptable witness."

I was taken away, locked in a cell for seventeen hours. In the early morning they released me without explanation. In the meantime, the ship had gone, and with it my luggage. I was stranded with only the clothes I was wearing. Luckily, I had not been deprived of either my passport or my wallet, and was well provided with money.

I had a shave, a wash and brush up, and looked carefully at my reflection. I needed a clean shirt, but the shops were not yet open; I would buy one later and change. For the moment my appearance was passable, or would be when I had got rid of the dead carnation. I meant to throw it into the gutter as I left the barber's shop, but a boy just outside offered to clean my shoes, and while he did so I asked him which was the best café. He pointed out one further along the same street; I walked on, liked the look of it, and sat down at one of the tables outside in the sun. At that hour the place was deserted. The solitary waiter on duty brought coffee and rolls on a tray, then returned to the dark interior, leaving me there alone. I drank the coffee, wondered what to do next, watched the passers-by: there were not many of them so early.

A girl went past carrying a basket of flowers, reminding me that, in the end, I had not disposed of the carnation. I tried to pull it out of my buttonhole, but the stem had been securely pinned by the steward. I turned back my lapel, peered down, felt about for the pin. Someone said: "Let me do that for you." I looked up; the flower girl was smiling at me. I seemed to have seen her face somewhere, I felt I already knew her and liked her. Having removed the carnation neatly, she prepared to replace it with one exactly the same from her basket. I was on the point of saying I did not want it, when something occurred to me and I kept silent. She fixed the fresh flower in my buttonhole and continued to stand beside me, although not as if she was merely waiting for payment. It looked as if my idea was correct, but I said nothing in case I was mistaken. I knew I had been right when she asked: "Is there anything else you'd like me to do?" I glanced round. The other tables were still deserted, the people on the pavement were out of earshot. She had put down her basket on a chair; I pretended to examine the flowers, picking up one bunch after another. To anyone watching, even through field-glasses, we would have appeared to be conducting a normal transaction. I said, "Certainly," although I wondered if she . . . But I had to find out without delay what had been going on in the world. "I've been at sea; out of touch. There are lots of things you can tell me."

I asked cautious questions, trying not to show the extent of my ignorance of the latest developments. It appeared that the situation at home was obscure and alarming, no precise information was coming through, the full extent of the disaster was not yet known. The warden of a northern country had escaped to the interior and joined forces with one of the various warlords, between whom hostilities had broken out.

I went on questioning her. She was always polite and friendly, and tried to be helpful. But her answers grew vague, she seemed afraid to commit herself. When one or two people drifted into the café and sat down near us, she said in a whisper: "You'll have to discuss these matters with somebody higher up. Do you want me to arrange it?" I agreed at once, but was rather skeptical about her power to do this. She told me to wait, picked up her basket, and rushed off down the street, half running. I thought I had probably seen the last of her, but ordered more coffee, waited; I had nothing else to do. The news she had given me of the warden's escape had relieved my mind, up to a point; it seemed likely, although by no means certain, that he had taken the girl with him. Time passed. There were plenty of people about now. I watched the street for my informant's return. Just as I had decided she was not coming back, I saw her hurrying toward me between the passers-by. As she came to my table she called out: "Here are the violets you wanted. I had to go all the way to the flower market for them. I'm afraid they're rather expensive." She was out of breath, but made her voice sound clear and gay for the benefit of the people round us. I saw that it would be no good trying to persuade her to stay, and asked: "How much?" She named a sum, I handed over the money. She thanked me with a charming smile, darted away, and disappeared in the crowd.

The stalks of the violets were wrapped in paper with words written on it. I was told where to find the man who might help me. The message was to be destroyed immediately. I bought a canvas bag with leather handles and straps to hold a few necessities, then booked at a hotel. When I had bathed and changed, I went to the office of the man named on the paper, who saw me at once. He too was wearing a red carnation. I should have to be careful.

I went straight to the point, there was no object in prevaricating. Naming the town from which the warden was operating, I asked if it was possible for me to get there. "No. Fighting is going on in the area, night raids on the town. No foreigners allowed in." "No exceptions?" He shook his head. "Anyway, there's no transport except for official personnel." After all these negative statements, I could only say: "Then you advise me to give up the idea?" "Officially speaking, yes." He looked at me slyly. "But not necessarily." His expression was more encouraging. "There's just a chance I may be able to help you. Anyway, I'll see what can be done. But don't count on it. It will probably be a few days before I have anything to report." I thanked him. We stood up and shook hands. He promised to notify me immediately he had any news.

I felt bored and restless. I had nothing to do. On the surface, the life of the town appeared normal, but underneath it was coming gradually to a standstill. The news from the north was scanty, confused, frightening. I realized that the destruction must have been on a gigantic scale. Little could have survived. The local broadcasters were cheerfully reassuring. It was the official policy, the population had to be kept calm. But these men actually seemed to believe their country would escape the cataclysm. I knew no country was safe, no matter how far removed from the present devastation, which would spread and spread, and ultimately cover the entire planet. Meanwhile, universal unrest was inevitable. It was the worst possible sign that war had already started, even though on a minor scale. That the more responsible governments were doing their utmost to pacify the belligerents only stressed the explosive nature of the situation, and the ominous threat of all-out warfare augmenting the present catastrophe. My anxiety about the girl, which had subsided slightly, revived again. She had gained nothing by escaping the destruction of one country, if she had gone to another about to engage in a full-scale war. I tried to believe the warden had sent her to safety, but knew too much about him to feel sure of that. It was absolutely essential for me to see him; otherwise I would never find out what had happened to her. I spent the evening in different bars, listening to the talk. His name was often mentioned, occasionally as a traitor to his own people, more frequently as a new, powerful, unknown influence on the war issue, a significant figure, a man to watch.

First thing in the morning the telephone rang in my room: someone wanted to see me. I said the person was to come up, hoping for a message from the official. "Hullo." The flower girl entered, smiling and unselfconscious. She saw my surprise. "Forgotten me already?" I said I had not expected her here. *She* looked surprised now. "But you know it's part of my job to bring your flower every morning." I kept quiet while she fixed the carnation. It was fatally easy to show my ignorance of the organization to which she belonged. I was curious about it, but afraid of giving myself away. It occurred to me that, by spending more time with her, I might pick up information without asking questions. Besides, she was young and attractive, I liked her natural, matter-of-fact behavior. It would relieve the boredom.

I invited her to dinner that evening. Her manners were charming, she acted in her usual engaging, unaffected way. Later we went to two nightclubs, danced. She was a delightful partner, seemed relaxed and talked freely, but told me nothing I did not already know. I took her back to the hotel with me; the porter looked the other way when we came in together. I was rather drunk. Her full skirt fell in a shining ring on the floor of my room. Very early in the morning, while I was still asleep, she left to go to the flower market; was back at breakfast time with a fresh carnation, bright eyed, cheerful and full of life, more attractive than she had been in the dark. I wanted to keep her with me, to anchor myself in the present through her. But she said: "No, I must go now, I have my work to do," then smiled in the friendliest way and promised to dance with me in the evening. I never saw her again.

The official sent for me while I was reading the papers. I hurried round to his office. He greeted me with a mysterious, conspiratorial air. "I've been able to arrange that matter for you. It'll be a bit of a rush." He grinned, pleased with himself, pleased to show me how he could manipulate events. I was surprised and excited. He went on: "A lorry happens to be leaving today with important replacements for the new transmitter that's going up on our side of the frontier. It's quite near the town you want. I've got you signed on as a foreign consultant. You can do your homework on the way. It's all in here." He handed me a thick folder full of papers, a travel permit on top, told me to be at the main post office in half an hour.

I thanked him profusely. He patted my arm. "Think nothing of it. Glad I could be useful." Withdrawing his hand, he touched the flower in my buttonhole and gave me a fright. Did he suspect something? If I had discovered nothing else about his organization, I at least knew now that it had considerable power. I was relieved when he said with a smile: "Hurry back and collect your things. You mustn't be late on any account. The driver has orders to leave on the dot, and he won't wait for anyone."

The room had been getting darker, a sudden storm had blown up. As his hand moved to the light, a livid flash and a crash came together, a splatter of rain hit the windows, and somebody wearing the long overcoat of a uniform entered and signed to him not to touch the switch. I could only just distinguish a big, heavily built man, whose massive shape seemed vaguely familiar. He stood talking to the official in undertones at the far end of the room, while I tried unsuccessfully to hear the low but heated discussion, of which I knew I was the subject, for they both kept glancing at me. It was obvious that I was being denigrated. Although the newcomer's face remained indistinct, between thunderclaps I could hear the accusing tone of his voice, but without being able to catch the words. He seemed already to have succeeded in discrediting me with the other man, who stood nearer the light, and showed signs of uneasiness and suspicion.

I was getting very uneasy myself. My position would be most unpleasant if he turned against me. Not only would I lose all hope of reaching the warden, but be shown up as having made use of the red carnation under false pretenses. There was a serious danger that I would be re-arrested and put in prison again.

I looked at my watch. Several minutes of the half hour had elapsed, and, feeling that I had to get out of the room quickly, I made an unobtrusive move to the door, opening it with my hand behind me.

A terrific flash split the air, luridly lit up a sudden flurry of movement, the folds of the overcoat swinging, its wearer pointing a gun. As I raised my hands, he half turned to shout above the exploding thunder to the man to whom he had been talking: "What did I tell you?" The momentary dividing of his attention gave me time to dive at his legs in a tackle I learned at school, while the shot went over my head. I did not manage to bring him down, but caught him off balance, hampered by the length of the coat. Before he could aim again, I had knocked the revolver out of his hand, sent it flying across the room. He came at me directly, threw his whole weight against me in a vicious onslaught, hitting hard with both fists. He was much heavier than I was, I almost fell. The door saved me; clinging to it, I heard steps coming along the passage. My opponent attacked me fiercely again, shouting to the official to retrieve his gun. Once he got hold of it I was done for. In desperation, I bashed the door into him, kicked him with all my strength, had the satisfaction of seeing him fold up before I swung round. Two new figures materialized in my way. I did not look at them, simply hurled them aside, one after the other, heard one fall with a cry, and the crash of the door as he fell against it. Nobody else tried to stop me; without looking back, I rushed down the corridor and out of the building. Thanks to the thunder, the shot could not have been heard beyond the adjoining office.

The storm continued to help me. I was not noticed outside, everyone had taken shelter from the torrential rain. The streets were swimming with water, I was wet through in a second, kept running as fast as I could, splashing along as if in a shallow stream. Luckily I knew where the main post office was and made straight for it. Instructions to detain me would have been telephoned to my hotel, and anyhow I had no time to go there. As it was, the lorry driver was starting his engine when I came up, waving my travel documents for him to see. He scowled at me, and jerked his thumb at the back of the vehicle. I made a final effort and scrambled up, subsided on to something extremely hard. Someone immediately shut out the rain and the daylight; there was a tremendous lurch; we were off. I was breathless, bruised all over and soaking wet, but I felt triumphant.

Four of us were crowded inside the lorry. It was dark, noisy and uncomfortable, like being in some sort of tent with planks to sit on, but not enough head room to sit up straight. Two on each plank, we crouched face to face in the congested darkness, among stacked packing-cases of different shapes and sizes. I hardly noticed the painful jolting, I was so relieved to be there, actually on my way, shut inside that cramped, comfortless, moving tent, where nobody could see me. The storm gradually died out, but the rain still streamed down, and eventually found its way through our canvas walk without damping my spirits. It could not possibly make me any wetter than I already was.

EIGHT

I tried to make friends with my companions, young fellows straight from a technical college; but they would not talk. They distrusted me because I was a foreigner. When I asked questions, they suspected me of trying to find out things that were to be kept secret, although I could see that they themselves knew no secrets. They were incredibly naïve. I felt I belonged to another dimension, and became silent. By degrees they forgot about me and started talking among themselves. They spoke of their work; of difficulties in assembling the transmitter. Lack of materials; lack of trained personnel; lack of funds; bad workmanship; unaccountable errors. I heard the word sabotage muttered back and forth. The work was far behind schedule. The transmitter should have been functioning at the end of the month. Now no one knew when it would be finished. Exhausted, I closed my eyes, stopped listening.

Now and again an odd sentence reached me. Once I realized I was the subject of their conversation; they thought I was asleep. "He's been sent to spy on us," one of them said. "To find out if we can be trusted. We must never tell him anything, never answer his questions." Their voices dropped, they were almost whispering. "I heard the professor say . . . They don't explain . . . Why send us to the danger zone when other people . . ." They were dissatisfied and uneasy, and could not give me any information. I need not waste my time on them.

Late at night we stopped at a small town. I knocked up a

shopkeeper, and, for the second time, provided myself with a few essentials: soap, a razor, a change of clothing. The place had only one garage: before we left in the morning, the driver insisted on buying up the entire stock of petrol. The owner protested indignantly; with supplies so restricted, he might not get any more. Our man ignored this, told him to empty the pumps, and, in response to further outraged protests, said: "Shut up, and get on with it! That's an order." Standing beside him, I remarked mildly that the next person expecting to fill up here would be in trouble. He gave me a scornful glance. "He's got more hidden away somewhere. They always have." The petrol cans were crammed into the back with the rest of the load, hardly leaving room for the four of us. I had the most uncomfortable place, over the back axle.

Flaps were rolled up, we could see out. We were driving toward a distant forest with a chain of mountains behind. A few miles from the town, the metaled road ended. Now there were only two narrow tarred strips for the wheels, as far apart as the width of the chassis. It got colder as we drove on; the climate was changing, like the character of the land. The edge of the forest was always in sight, gradually coming nearer: we passed less and less cultivation, fewer and fewer people and villages. I began to see the sense of storing the petrol. The road got steadily worse, full of ruts and holes. Progress was difficult, slow, the driver kept swearing. When even the tarred strips came to an end, I leaned over and tapped his shoulder, offered to take turns with him at the wheel. Rather to my surprise, he agreed.

I had a more comfortable seat beside him, but found it an effort to handle the heavy lorry. I had never driven one before, and, until I got used to it, had to concentrate on what I was doing. It was necessary to stop at intervals to remove fallen rocks or tree trunks that blocked the way. The first time this happened, I prepared to climb out to help the others, who had already jumped down from the back and were struggling to shift the obstruction. I felt a light touch and

looked round. The driver's head made a just perceptible negative movement. My ability to drive the truck had apparently
raised me above such duties in his estimation.

I offered him a cigarette. He accepted. I ventured a com-
ment on the state of the road. As the transmitter was so
important and involved so much traffic, I could not understand why a decent road had not been made. He said: "We
can't afford new roads. We asked the other nations associated with us in the undertaking to contribute, but they
refused." Frowning, he gave me a sidelong glance to see
where my sympathies lay. I said in a non-committal tone
that this seemed unfair. "Just because we're a small, impov-
erished country, they've treated us badly all along the line."
He could not suppress his resentment. "The transmitter
could never have been built here at all if we hadn't donated
the site. They should remember that we made the whole
thing possible. We sacrifice a piece of our land for the general good, but get nothing in return. They won't even send
ground troops to help to protect the position. It's their
unsympathetic attitude that creates bad feeling." He spoke
bitterly. I could feel his grudge against the big powers.
"You're a stranger . . . I shouldn't be saying such things to
you." He looked at me with anxiety: I assured him I was
not an informer.

Now that he had begun, he wanted to go on talking. I
encouraged him to tell me about himself; it was the way to
get him to speak of the things I was interested in. When the
project first started, he had driven parties of workers along
this road; they used to sing on the way. "You remember the
old formula—'all men of goodwill to unite in the task of
world recovery and against the forces of destruction.' They
made the words into a sort of part song, men and women
singing them together. It was inspiring to listen. We were all
full of enthusiasm in those days. Now everything's different." I asked what had gone wrong. "Too many setbacks,
delays, disappointments. The work would have been finished long ago if we'd had the materials. But everything had

to come from abroad; from countries with different standards of measurement. Sometimes parts did not fit together; whole consignments had to go back. You can imagine the effect of such incidents on young enthusiasts, eager to get the job done." It was the usual story of mistakes and muddles due to different ideologies, lack of direct contact. I thanked him for speaking frankly about these matters. A ball neatly volleyed, back bounced the cliché: "Contact between individuals is the first step toward a better understanding between peoples."

I seemed to have won his confidence. He became quite friendly, told me about his girl, showed snapshots of her playing with a dog. I considered it unwise to let people know that I carried a sum of money, so drew his attention to something at the roadside while I quickly took out of my wallet the photograph I still kept there of the girl standing beside a lake. I showed it to him, saying that she had disappeared and that I was looking for her. Without any special feeling, he commented: "Wonderful hair. You're in luck." I asked rather sharply whether he would think himself lucky if his girl had vanished off the face of the earth, and he had the grace to look slightly embarrassed. I put the photo away, asked if he'd ever seen hair like that. "No, never." He shook his head emphatically. "Most of our women are dark." It was no use talking to him about her.

We changed places. I was tired after my stint of driving and shut my eyes. When I opened them again he had a gun lying across his knees. I asked what he expected to shoot. "We're getting near the frontier. It's dangerous here. Enemies everywhere." "But this country is neutral." "What's neutral? It's just a word." He added mysteriously: "Besides, there are various kinds of enemies." "Such as?" "Saboteurs. Spies. Gangsters. All sorts of scoundrels who flourish in times of disorder." I asked if he thought the lorry would be attacked. "It has happened. The stuff we've got on board is urgently needed. If they've got to hear about it they may try to stop us."

I brought out my automatic, saw him glancing at it with interest, evidently impressed by the foreign weapon. We had just entered the forest. He seemed nervous. "This is where the danger begins." The tall trees had long gray beards of moss hanging down from their branches, forming opaque screens. It looked a good place to hide. The light was starting to fade, and what was left of it fell on the road, so that it was easy to imagine invisible eyes watching us. I kept a lookout for gunmen, but had other things on my mind.

I spoke to the driver about the warden. He knew only what he had read in the newspapers. The distance to his headquarters from the transmitter was about twenty miles. "Can one go there?" "Go there?" He stared at me blankly. "Of course not. It's enemy country. And they've destroyed the road, blocked the pass. There can't be much of the town left, anyhow. We hear the guns pounding it at night." He was more interested in reaching our destination in daylight. "We must get out of the forest before dark. We'll just make it, with any luck." He drove furiously, the lorry bounced and skidded over loose stones.

I was too depressed to go on talking. The situation was hopeless. I needed the girl, could not live without her. But I should never be able to find her. There was no road to the town, I should never get there, it was impossible. In any case, the place was under constant bombardment and must have been destroyed. There was no object in going there. She had either left or been killed long ago. I felt in despair. I seemed to have come all this way for nothing.

The site for the transmitter had been carefully chosen, high up, surrounded by forest, backed by mountains, an easy place to defend against ground attack. They had cleared the area immediately round the installation, but the trees were not far away. We lived in prefabricated buildings that let in the rain. Everything felt damp to the touch. The floors were concrete, always covered in mud. Everywhere we walked became a morass. Everyone grumbled about the discomfort and the poor quality of the food.

Something had gone wrong with the weather. It should have been hot, dry, sunny; instead it rained all the time, there was a dank chill in the air. Thick white mists lay entangled in the tops of the forest trees; the sky was a perpetually steaming cauldron of cloud. The forest creatures were disturbed, and departed from their usual habits. The big cats lost their fear of man, came up to the buildings, prowled round the transmitter; strange unwieldy birds flopped overhead. I got the impression that birds and animals were seeking us out for protection against the unknown danger we had unloosed. The abnormalities in their behavior seemed ominous.

To pass the time and for want of something better to do, I organized the work on the transmitter. It was not far from completion, but the workers had grown discouraged and apathetic. I assembled them and spoke of the future. The belligerents would listen and be impressed by the impartial accuracy of our reports. The soundness of our arguments would convince them. Peace would be restored. Danger of universal conflict averted. This was to be the final reward of their labors. In the meantime, I divided them into teams, arranged competitions, awarded prizes to those who worked best. Soon we were ready to start broadcasting. I recorded events on both sides with equal respect for truth, put out programs on world peace, urged an immediate ceasefire. The minister wrote, congratulating me on my work.

I could not make up my mind whether to cross the frontier or to stay where I was. I did not think the girl could be alive in the demolished town. If she had been killed there it was pointless to go. If she was safe somewhere else there was no point in going either. Considerable personal risk was involved. Although a non-combatant, I was liable to be shot as a spy, or imprisoned indefinitely.

But I was becoming tired of the work here now that everything was running smoothly. I was tired of trying to keep dry in the perpetual rain, tired of waiting to be overtaken by ice. Day by day the ice was creeping over the curve of the earth, unimpeded by seas or mountains. Without haste or pause, it was steadily moving nearer, entering and flattening cities, filling craters from which boiling lava had poured. There was no way of stopping the icy giant battalions, marching in relentless order across the world, crushing, obliterating, destroying everything in their path.

I made up my mind to go. Without telling anyone, in the drenching rain, I drove to the blocked pass, and from there found my way over the tree-covered mountains on foot. I had only a pocket compass to guide me. It took me several hours of climbing and struggling through wet vegetation to reach the frontier station, where I was detained by the guard.

NINE

I asked to be taken to the warden. He had lately moved his headquarters to a different town. An armored car drove me there; two soldiers with submachine guns came too, "for my protection." It was still raining. We crashed through the downpour under heavy black clouds which shut out the last of the day. Darkness was falling as we entered the town. The headlights showed the familiar scene of havoc, rubble, ruins, blank spaces, all glistening in rain. The streets were full of troops. The least damaged buildings were used as barracks.

I was taken into a heavily guarded place and left in a small room where two men were waiting. The three of us were alone: they stared at me, but said nothing. We waited in silence. There was only the sound of the rain beating down outside. They sat together on one bench; I, wrapped in my coat, on another. That was all the furniture in the room, which had not been cleaned. Thick dust lay over everything.

After a while they began to converse in whispers. I gathered that they had come about some post that was vacant. I stood up, started pacing backward and forward. I was restless, but knew I should have to wait. I was not listening to what the others were saying, but one raised his voice so that I had to hear. He was certain that he would get the job. He boasted: "I've been trained to kill with my hands. I can kill the strongest man with three fingers. I've learned the points in the body where you can kill easily. I can break a block of wood with the side of my hand." His words depressed me.

This was the kind of man who was wanted now. The two were presently called to an interview and I was left waiting alone. I was prepared to have to wait a long time.

It was not so long before a guard came to conduct me to the officers' mess. The warden was sitting at the head of the high table. Other long tables were more crowded. I was to sit at his table, but not near him, at the far end. We should be too far apart to talk comfortably. Before taking my seat, I went up to salute him. He looked surprised and did not return my greeting. I noticed all the men sitting round immediately leaned together and began speaking in under-tones, glancing furtively at me. I seemed to have made an unfavorable impression. I had assumed he would remember me, but he appeared not to know who I was. To remind him of our former connection might make things worse, so I sat down in my distant place.

I could hear him talking amiably to the officers near him. Their conversation was of arrests and escapes. I was not interested until he told the story of his own flight, involving a big car, a snowstorm, crashing frontier gates, bullets, a girl. He never once looked in my direction or took any notice of me.

From time to time troops could be heard marching past outside. Suddenly there was an explosion. Part of the ceiling collapsed and the lights went out. Hurricane lamps were brought and put on the table. They showed fragments of plaster lying among the dishes. The food was ruined, uneat-able, covered in dust and debris. It was taken away. A long and tedious wait followed; then finally bowls of hard-boiled eggs were put down in front of us. Intermittent explosions continued to shake the building, a haze of whitish dust hung in the air, everything was gritty to touch.

The warden was playing a game of surprising me. He beck-oned at the end of the meal. "I enjoyed your broadcasts. You have a gift for that sort of thing." I was astonished that he knew of the work I had been doing. His voice was friendly, he spoke to me as an equal, and just for a moment I felt identified with him in an obscure sort of intimacy. He went on to say I had timed my arrival well. "Our transmitter will soon be in operation, and yours will be put out of action." I had always told the authorities we needed a more powerful installation; that it was only a question of time before the existing apparatus was jammed by a stronger one. He assumed that I had heard this was about to happen, and had defected accordingly. He wanted me to broadcast propaganda for him, which I agreed to do, if he would do something for me. "Still the same thing?" "Yes." He looked at me in amusement, but suspicion flashed in his eyes. Nevertheless he remarked casually, "Her room's on the floor above; we may as well pay her a visit," and led the way out. But when I said, "I have to deliver a personal message; could I see her alone?" he did not reply.

We went down one passage, up some stairs and along another. The beam of his powerful torch played on floors littered with rubbish. Footprints showed in the dust; I looked among them for her smaller prints. He opened a door into a dimly lit room. She jumped up. Her white startled face; big eyes staring at me under glittering hair. "You again!" She stood rigid, held the chair in front of her as for protection, hands clenched on the back, knuckles standing out white. "What do you want?" "Only to talk to you." Looking from one of us to the other, she accused: "You're in league together." I denied it: although in a strange way there seemed to be some truth in the charge . . . "Of course you are. He wouldn't bring you here otherwise."

The warden approached her, smiling. I had never seen him look so benevolent. "Come now, that's not a very kind way to greet an old friend. Can't we all have a friendly talk? You've never told me how you first got to know each other." It was clear that he had no intention of leaving us alone. I gazed at her silently, could not talk to her in front of him. His personality was too dominant, his influence too strong. In his presence she was frightened, antagonistic. Barriers were created. I was distracted myself. No wonder he smiled.

I might as well not have found her. A distant explosion shook the walls; she watched the white dust float down from the ceiling. For the sake of saying something, I asked if the bombing disturbed her. Her face blank, her bright hair shimmering, she silently moved her head in a way that meant anything, nothing.

The warden said: "I've tried to persuade her to go to a safer place, but she refuses to leave." He smiled complacently, showing me his power over her. I found it hard to accept. I looked round the room: the chair, a small mirror, a bed, paperbacks on the table, dust everywhere, fallen plaster thick on the floor. Her gray loden coat hung from a hook. I saw no other personal belongings except a comb and a square of chocolate in torn silver paper. I turned away from the man and addressed her directly, trying to speak as if he was not there. "You don't seem very comfortable here. Why not go to a hotel, somewhere further away from the fighting?" She did not answer, shrugged her shoulders slightly. A silence followed.

Troops marched past under the window. He went across, opened the shutters a crack and looked down. I muttered hurriedly, "I only want to help you," moved my hand toward hers, which was snatched back. "I don't trust you. I don't believe a word you say." Her eyes were wide and defiant. I knew I would never succeed in making contact with her while he was in the room. Nothing was to be gained by staying longer. I left.

Outside the door, I heard his laugh, his step on the floorboards, his voice: "What have you got against that one?" Then her voice, changed, blurred with tears, high pitched, hysterical. "He's a liar. I know he's working with you. You're both the same, selfish, treacherous, cruel. I wish I'd never met either of you, I hate you both! One day I'll go . . . you won't see me again . . . ever!" I walked on down the passage, stumbling over the rubble, kicking it aside. I had not thought of providing myself with a torch.

For the next few days I considered taking her away from

him to a neutral country. Theoretically it was quite possible. Occasional ships still called at the local port. It was a matter of speed, secrecy and exact timing. Success depended on getting to sea before we were followed. I began making cautious inquiries. The answers could be bought. The difficulty was that no one could be trusted. The person I was paying for information might sell my questions to somebody in the warden's pay. This made the whole thing highly dangerous. I was nervous; I could not afford to take such risks; nevertheless, the risk had to be run.

Voices whispered secrets: names, addresses, destinations, departures. "Go to . . . ask for . . . hold yourself in instant readiness . . . documents . . . proof . . . ample funds . . ." I needed to speak to her before taking my plans a stage further. I went to her room, heard a shot, paid no attention; shooting was going on in the streets all the time. The man emerged, shut the door behind him. I said I wanted to see her. "You can't." He turned the key, dropped it into his pocket, threw a pistol down on the table. "She's dead." A knife went through me. All other deaths in the world were outside; this one was in my body, like a bayonet, like my own. "Who killed her?" Only I could do that. When he said, "I did," my hand moved, touched the gun, the barrel was hot. I could have seized it and shot him. It would have been easy. He made no move to prevent me, stood motionless, gazing at me. I looked back at him, at his face with its arrogant bone structure; our eyes met.

In an indescribable way our looks tangled together. I seemed to be looking at my own reflection. Suddenly I was entangled in utmost confusion, not sure which of us was which. We were like halves of one being, joined in some mysterious symbiosis. I fought to retain my identity, but all my efforts failed to keep us apart. I continually found I was not myself, but him. At one moment I actually seemed to be wearing his clothes. I fled from the room in utter confusion: afterward did not know what had happened, or if anything had.

On another occasion he met me at the door of the room, said at once: "You're too late. The bird's flown." He was grinning, his face wore an expression of naked malice. "She's gone. Run away. Disappeared." My fists clenched. "You sent her away so that I shouldn't see her. You've deliberately kept us apart." I started toward him in fury. Then again our looks tangled, confusion came back; a wider confusion, not of identity only, but also of time and place. Cold blue eyes flashing, the blue flash of a ring, curved cold strangler's fingers. He had fought bears and strangled them with his hands. Physically I was no match . . . As I left, I heard his voice jeering: "That's more sensible."

I went into an empty room. I needed time in which to collect myself. I was disturbed, I longed for the girl, could not bear to have lost her. I thought of the journey I had been planning with her beside me, which would now never take place. My face was wet as with rain, drops ran down into my mouth, tasted salt. I covered my eyes with my handkerchief, brought myself under control by a violent effort.

I should have to start searching for her all over again. The repetition was like a curse. I thought of placid blue seas, tranquil islands, far away from war. I thought of the Indris, those happy creatures, symbols of life in peace, on a higher plane. I could clear out, go to them. No, that was impossible. I was tied to her. I thought of the ice moving across the world, casting its shadow of creeping death. Ice cliffs boomed in my dreams, indescribable explosions thundered and boomed, icebergs crashed, hurled huge boulders into the sky like rockets. Dazzling ice stars bombarded the world with rays, which splintered and penetrated the earth, filling earth's core with their deadly coldness, reinforcing the cold of the advancing ice. And always, on the surface, the indestructible ice-mass was moving forward, implacably destroying all life. I felt a fearful sense of pressure and urgency, there was no time to lose, I was wasting time; it was a race between me and the ice. Her albino hair illumi-

nated my dreams, shining brighter than moonlight. I saw
the dead moon dance over the icebergs, as it would at the
end of our world, while she watched from the tent of her
glittering hair.

I dreamed of her whether I was asleep or awake. I heard
her cry: "One day I'll go . . . you won't see me again . . ."
She had gone from me already. She had escaped. She hurried along a street in an unknown town. She looked different, less anxious, more confident. She knew exactly where
she was going, she did not hesitate once. In a huge official
building she made straight for a room so crowded she could
hardly open the door. Only her extreme slimness enabled
her to slip between the many tall silent figures, unnaturally
silent, fantastically tall, whose faces were all averted from
her. Her anxiety started to come back when she saw them
towering over her, surrounding her like dark trees. She felt
small and lost among them, quickly became afraid. Her
confidence had vanished; it had never been real. Now she
only wanted to escape from that place: her eyes darted from
side to side, saw no door, no way out. She was trapped. The
faceless black treeforms pressed closer, extended arm-
branches, imprisoning her. She looked down, but was still
imprisoned. Filled trouser-legs, solid tree trunks, stood all
around. The floor had become dark earth, full of roots and
boles. Quickly looking up at the window, she saw only
white weaving meshes of snow, shutting out the world. The
known world excluded, reality blotted out, she was alone
with threatening nightmare shapes of trees or phantoms,
tall as firs growing in snow.

Global conditions were worsening. There was no sign of
destruction coming to a halt, and its inexorable progress
induced general demoralization. It was more impossible
than ever to find out what was really happening, impossible
to know what to believe. No reliable source of information
existed. Very little news of any description came from
abroad; none whatsoever from once-prominent states which

had simply dropped out of existence. More than any other single factor, it was the implacable spread of these unnerving areas of total silence that undermined public morale.

In certain countries civil unrest had resulted in the army taking command. A worldwide swing toward militarism had taken place during recent months, with deplorable and brutalizing effects. Frequent clashes occurred between civilians and the armed forces. The killing of police and soldiers, with retributory executions, had become commonplace.

As was to be expected, in the absence of any genuine news, fantastic rumors kept circulating. Monstrous epidemics, appalling famines, were said to have broken out in remote districts, fearsome deviations to have occurred from the genetic norm. Stocks of thermonuclear weapons, previously supposed to have been destroyed, were periodically reported to be in the possession of this or that power. Persistent rumors concerned the existence of a self-detonating cobalt bomb, timed, at a preset, unknown moment, to destroy all life, while leaving inanimate objects intact. Spying and counter-spying went on everywhere. There were growing acute shortages in all countries, food riots followed as a matter of course. The lawless element in the population was much in evidence, decent people were terrorized. The death penalty imposed for looting had little or no effect as a deterrent.

I got news of the girl indirectly. She was alive, in a certain town, in another country. I was almost sure the place was in the area of immediate danger, although there was no means of checking the point, since all reference to the advancing ice was forbidden. By intense persistence and extensive bribery, I managed to board a ship traveling in that direction. The captain wanted to make money fast, and for a large sum agreed to put in at the port I named.

We arrived. It was early morning, unbelievably cold, dark when it should have been light. No sky, no clouds, they were hidden by falling snow. It was not a morning like other mornings, but what it was: an unnatural freezing of day into darkness, spring into arctic winter. I went to say good-bye to the captain, who asked if I had changed my mind about going ashore. I said I had not. "Then for God's sake get going. Don't keep us hanging about." He was angry, antagonistic. We parted without more words.

I went on deck with the first officer. The air stung like acid. It was the breath of ice, of the polar regions, almost unbreathable. It scarified the skin, seared the lungs; but the body quickly adjusted itself to this stringency. The density of the snow created a curious fog-like gloom in the upper air. Everything was obscured by the small flakes falling ceaselessly out of the shrouded sky. The cold scalded my hands when I collided with iced-up parts of the ship's superstructure, which only became visible when it was too late to avoid them. In the silence I noticed a rhythmic vibration below, and spoke to my escort: "The engines; they haven't stopped." For some reason it seemed surprising. "You bet they haven't. The skipper can't wait to turn the ship round. He's been cursing you for days for making us put in here." The man showed the same antagonism as the captain, plus a disagreeable curiosity which came out now. "Why the devil *have* you come, anyhow?" "That's my business." In unfriendly silence we reached the rail. It was cased in thick ice, a rope ladder dangling from it toward the sound of a motor running below. Before I had time to look down, he swung his leg over. "Harbor's frozen. We've got to put you ashore by launch." While he quickly descended with practiced ease, I followed more awkwardly, clinging on with both hands, blinded by the snow. I did not see who pulled me into the rocking launch, or who pushed me toward a seat, as it immediately shot forward. Traveling at full speed, it plunged and reared continually like a bucking horse, sheets of spray flew over the roof of the little cabin. There was too much noise for voices to be audible; but I could feel the almost murderous hostility of those on board, all hating me for keeping them here in danger when they might have been on the way to safety. To them my behavior must have seemed perverse and utterly senseless. I began to wonder myself whether it made any sense, sitting huddled up in my coat, in the brutal paralyzing cold.

A sudden long-drawn-out yell startled me; it was really more of a howl. The officer jumped up, shouted back through a megaphone, then resumed his seat with the words: "One-way traffic." Seeing that I did not understand, he added, "Plenty going the other way," and pointed ahead.

A confused indistinct commotion revealed itself as a ship, motionless in the midst of the feverish activity of small boats seething round it. In frantic competition, they fought to get near enough for their occupants to climb aboard. There was not room for all. Spectators crowded the rails of the ship as if at a racecourse, watching the collisions and capsizings below. Those in the boats had probably lived easily and been unaccustomed to danger, for they battled clumsily for their lives, with a sort of headlong terror, wasting their strength in useless jostling and surging. One boat floated upside down, surrounded by frenzied hands and arms struggling out of the water. The people in the next boat swarmed over it, hit out, kicked, stamped on the clinging hands, beat off the drowning. Even the most powerful swimmer could not survive long in that freezing sea. Several of the overcrowded, unskillfully handled boats turned over and sank. Some broke up after colliding. In those that remained afloat, the passengers crushed and trampled each other in senseless panic, drove off clutching swimmers with oars. People already dying were battered and beaten. The muffled uproar of screams, thuds, splashes, continued long after the scene was hidden behind the snow. I recalled polite voices announcing over the air that people were desperate, fighting to get away from the threatened countries to safer regions.

The frozen harbor was a gray-white expanse, dotted with black abandoned hulks, embedded immovably in the ice. Banks of solid ice edged the narrow channel of blackish water, fringed with grinning icicle-teeth. I jumped ashore, snow blew out in great fans, the launch disappeared from sight. There were no good-byes.

TEN

It could have been any town, in any country. I recognized nothing. Snow covered all landmarks with the same white padding. Buildings were changed into anonymous white cliffs.

A confused disturbance, shouts, the noise of wood splintering and glass breaking came from one of the streets where looting was going on. A crowd had broken into the shops. They had no leader, no fixed objective. They were just a disorderly mob surging about in search of excitement and booty, frightened, hungry, hysterical, violent. They kept fighting among themselves, picking up anything that could be used as a weapon, snatching each other's spoils, taking possession of all they could lay hands on, even the most useless objects, then dropping them and running after some other plunder. What they could not take away they destroyed. They had a senseless mania for destruction, for tearing to shreds, smashing to smithereens, trampling underfoot.

A senior army officer appeared in the street and blew a whistle to summon the police. Striding toward the looters, he shouted orders in a fierce military voice, blew repeated blasts on the whistle. His face was dark with rage, framed by the astrakhan collar of his fine overcoat. The main mass of the crowd fled at the sight of him. But some, bolder than the rest, stayed skulking among the wreckage. Furious, he strode toward them, threatened them with his cane, shouted to them to clear off, swore at them. They took no notice at first; then formed a rough circle, rushed at him from several points simultaneously, in groups of three or four together.

He pulled out his revolver, fired it over their heads. A mistake: he should have fired at them. They swarmed round him, trying to snatch the weapon. The police were a long time coming. There was a scuffle. In the course of it, either by accident or intention, the gun was dropped through a grating. Its owner was a man in his late fifties, tall, vigorous. But I could see him panting. They were young toughs with faces of a sinister blankness. They attacked cunningly, with bits of metal and broken glass, pieces of smashed furniture, whatever came to hand. He fended them off with his cane, keeping his back to a wall. Their numbers and their persistence were gradually wearing him down; his movements were getting slower. A stone was thrown. Then a shower of stones. One of them knocked his cap off. The sight of his hairless skull produced ribald shouting, and for a second he seemed disconcerted. They took advantage of this, closed in, set on him like a pack of wolves. Blood trickling down his face, back to the wall, he still managed to fight them off. Then I saw something flash: someone had used a knife. Others followed suit. He clutched his chest, blindly staggered forward. The moment he left the wall he was done for, they were on him from every side. They knocked him down, sprang on top of him, tore his coat off, beat his head on the frozen ground, stamped on him, kicked him, slashed his face with chains. Finally he lay still on the snow. He had had absolutely no chance. It was murder.

It was not my affair, but I could not see it and stand there doing nothing. They were society's dregs, they would never have dared come near him in normal times, far less touch him. A little jeering fellow had draped himself in the fine overcoat and was dancing about, tripping over the trailing hem. I was disgusted, furious. In uncontrollable fury I charged at him, stripped off the coat, twisted his arms, punched and pummel him, slung him across the pavement, heard a satisfactory crunch when his screaming face hit the wall. Turning, I confronted a man twice his size, half saw a boot flick out. Acute pain in my leg made me stumble: I recovered just in time to see his arm swing up in a practiced curve, and reacted as I had been trained. A textbook fall; flat on my back, one foot locking his ankle, I caught the glint of the falling knife, as my other leg bashed the trapped kneecap until it cracked. In a moment I would have the entire crew swarming all over me. I had no more chance than the officer against the lot of them with their knives; but I meant to do some damage before they finished me off. Suddenly there were shots, shouts, the sound of running feet: the police had arrived at last. I watched them chase the looters round a corner into another street; then limped over to the man on the ground.

He lay on his back, bleeding from many wounds. Not much past the prime of life, he had looked impressive, a tall, vital, imposing man, still desirable physically. Now his nose had been flattened, his mouth slit at the corners, one eye was half out of its socket, his whole face and head discolored with blood and dirt, the shapes lost and distorted. Blood was everywhere. They had almost torn off his right arm. He did not move, I could not see his breathing. I knelt down, opened his tunic, his shirt, put my hand on his chest. The heart was not to be felt, and my hand came out sticky with blood. I wiped it on my handkerchief, then went for his coat, spread it over him, hiding the mess. I wanted to leave him some dignity. He was a stranger to whom I had never spoken; but he was my sort of man; we were not like that rabble. It was an outrage that they should have killed him. They must have cringed before him in his strength and power. This was how they treated him when they caught him alone, no longer young, and at a disadvantage. It was disgusting. I regretted not having inflicted more punishment on them.

I remembered the revolver, stooped over the grating. There was just room for my fingers between the bars, and I pulled it up, put it into my pocket, moved on. I was still limping badly, my leg was painful. Suddenly someone shouted, a shot zipped past. I stopped, waited until the police overtook me. "Who are you? What are you doing here? Why did you touch the body? It's not allowed." Before I could answer, there was a rasping noise and a ground-floor window burst open, dislodging masses of snow from the sill, a woman's head stuck out just beside me. "This man's brave. He deserves a medal. I saw what happened. He rushed in and tackled the lot of them single-handed, although they had knives and he was unarmed. I saw everything from this window." A policeman wrote down her name and address in his notebook.

Their attitude became more friendly; but they insisted that I should go to the station and make a report. One of them took my arm. "It's only in the next street. You look as if you could do with some first aid." I had to go in. It was unfortunate: I did not want to give an account of myself and my movements and motives. Besides, the revolver would make things awkward if it was noticed; they were bound to recognize the service pattern. When I took off my coat, I arranged it carefully so that the bulge did not show. They patched me up, strapped my leg with plaster. I had a wash, drank some strong coffee with rum in it. The chief inter-viewed me alone. He glanced at my papers, but gave the impression of being preoccupied with something else: it was not possible to ask if he had any precise information about the advancing ice. We exchanged cigarettes, discussed the food problem. He said rations were short, and distributed according to the value to the community of each individual's work: "No work, no food." His face showed signs of strain while he was talking; the crisis must be nearer than I had supposed. Planning my questions deliberately, I asked about refugees. Gangs of starving fugitives from the ice were a problem in all the surviving countries. "If they're able to work we let them stay. We need all the workers we can get." I said: "Doesn't that create difficulties? How do you manage to house them all?" "There are camps for the men. We put the women in hostels." I had been leading up to this point. Pretending to take a professional interest, I inquired: "Would

I be allowed to look over one of these places?" "Why not?" His smile was tired. I could not tell whether he was exceptionally civilized or merely indifferent. Before I left he gave me an address. Things had turned out very much better than I had expected. I had got the information I wanted, and a good army revolver.

I went to look for her. It was snowing again, the wind was colder and stronger. The streets were deserted, there was nobody to direct me. I thought I had found the house, but saw no sign. Perhaps I was too late: through an unaccountable failure of impulse had waited too long . . . I tried the street doors as I passed them; they were all locked.

The door of one house was unfastened. I entered without hesitation. Inside, the place was bare and shabby, had the look of an institution. The rooms were unheated. She sat wearing her gray overcoat, her legs wrapped in something that looked like a curtain. As soon as she saw me she threw this aside and sprang up. "You! I suppose he sent you— didn't you get my message?" "No one sent me. What message?" "I left a message telling you not to follow me." I said I had not received it, but if I had it would have made no difference, I should have come just the same. Her big distrustful eyes gazed at me, indignant and frightened. "I don't want anything to do with either of you." I ignored this. "You can't stay here alone." "Why not? I'm getting on all right." I asked what she was doing. "Working." "How much do they pay you?" "We get our food." "No money?" "Sometimes people are given money when they've worked specially hard." Defensively she went on: "I'm too thin for the really hard jobs. They say I haven't got enough stamina." I had been watching her: she looked half-starved, as if for some time she had not had enough to eat. Her thin wrists had always fascinated me; now I could scarcely take my eyes off them, emerging like sticks from the heavy sleeves. Instead of inquiring into the nature of the work she was doing, I asked her plans for the future. When she snapped: "Why should I tell you?" I knew that she had no plans. I said I very much wished she would look on me as a friend. "Why? I've no reason to. Anyhow, I don't need friends. I can manage alone." I told her I had come hoping to take her away with me to a place where life would be easier, somewhere in a better climate. I felt her beginning to weaken, waved my hand at the window covered in heavy frost, snow banked on the sill to half its whole height. "Haven't you had enough of the cold?" She could no longer hide her nervousness, her hands twisted together. I added: "Besides, you're in the danger zone here." Her face was starting to have its bruised look, she was gradually losing control. "What danger?" The pupils of her eyes dilated as I watched her. "The ice . . ." I meant to say more, but the two words were sufficient. Her whole appearance indicated fear, she began to tremble.

I moved closer to her, touched her hand. She jerked it away. "Don't do that!" I held a fold of her coat, looked at her angry, frightened face of a child betrayed, the look of faint bruising round the eyes like a child that has cried a long time. "Leave me alone!" She tried to drag the heavy material out of my hand. "Go away!" I did not move. "Then I'll go!" She tore herself free, dashed to the door, threw her whole weight against it. It crashed open so violently that she lost her balance and fell. The bright hair spread on the floor, quicksilver, brilliant, stirring, alive, on the dark, dull, dead, dirty floor. I picked her up. She struggled, gasped: "Let me go! I hate you, I hate you!" She had no strength at all. It was like holding a struggling kitten. I shut the door and turned the key in the lock.

I waited a few days, although waiting was difficult. It was time to go. It was only a matter of hours before a disaster of the magnitude. In spite of the secrecy which enveloped the subject, news must have leaked out. Agitated activity suddenly spread through the town. From my window I watched a young man running from house to house, delivering a message of terror. In an astonishingly short time, minutes only, the street was full of people carrying bags and bundles.

Disorganized, and showing every sign of acute fear, they set off in great haste, some going one way and some another. They seemed to have no definite destination or plan, just the one overwhelming urge to fly from the town. I was surprised that the authorities took no action. Presumably they had failed to evolve a workable scheme for evacuation, so simply decided to let things take their course. The chaotic exodus was disturbing to watch. Everybody seemed on the verge of panic. People clearly thought I was mad to sit in a bar instead of preparing for flight. Their fears were infectious; the atmosphere of impending catastrophe made me uneasy, and I was thankful to get the message I was expecting. A ship was about to anchor outside the harbor, somewhere beyond the ice. It was the last one that would call, and it would stay at anchor for one hour only.

I went to the girl, told her this was our last chance, and that she had to come. She refused, refused to stand up. "I'm not going anywhere with you. I don't trust you. I shall stay here where I'm free." "Free for what? To starve? To be frozen to death?" I lifted her off the chair bodily, stood her on her feet. "I won't go—you can't force me." She backed away, wide eyed, and stood against the wall, waiting for someone or something to rescue her. I lost patience, dragged her out of the building, went on holding her arm; I had to pull her along.

It was snowing so hard I could barely see to the other side of the street; a stark, white, deathly, pre-polar scene. The arctic wind drove floods of snow past us like feathers. Walking was difficult, the wind slammed the snow in our faces, hurled it at us from different sides, whirled it round us in crazy spirals. Everything was muffled, blurred, indistinct, not a person to be seen. Then suddenly six mounted policemen rode out of the blizzard, hooves soundless and bridles jingling. The girl cried, "Help!" when she saw them. She thought they would save her, tried to struggle free, made an imploring gesture with her free hand. I held on to her tight, kept her close beside me. The men laughed and whistled at us as they passed, disappearing in the blowing white. She burst into tears.

I heard a bell ringing, slowly coming nearer. An old priest shuffled round the corner, black-cowled, bent double against the storm, leading a rabble of people. The bell was the sort used to call schoolchildren from the playground; as he walked, he kept ringing it feebly. When his arm tired, he gave it a brief rest, calling out in a quavering voice: "Sauve qui peut!" Some of his followers took up the cry, chanting it like a dirge: one or two paused long enough to bang on the doors they were passing. From some of the houses muffled figures crept out to join them. I wondered where they were going; it did not look as if they would get very far. They were all old and infirm, decrepit. The young and able-bodied had left them behind. They moved with weak tottering steps in a slow, shambling procession, their movements uncoordinated, their faded faces reddened by the blast.

The girl kept stumbling in the deep snow. I had to half carry her, although I could hardly breathe. The frost tore my breath away, tried to stop me breathing; my breath froze in icicles on my collar. The frozen mucous membranes plugged my nose with ice. Each time I took a mouthful of polar air I coughed and gasped. It seemed hours before we got to the harbor. She renewed her feeble struggles at the sight of the boat, cried: "You can't do this to me . . ." I pushed her in, jumped in after her, seized the oars, shoved off, started rowing with all my might.

Voices screamed after us, but I ignored them; she was my one concern. The open channel had narrowed considerably, its edges frozen; soon it would be solid ice. Extraordinary loud, long cracks, like shots, like thunderclaps, came from the thickening ice of the harbor. My face felt raw, my hands were blue and burning with cold, but I kept on rowing toward the ship, through the churning white of the blizzard, through flying spray, booming ice, shrieks, crashes, blood. A small boat foundered beside us, the water seethed with frantically lashing limbs. Desperate drowning fingers clawed at the gunwale; I beat them off. A pair of lovers floated past, locked together by frozen arms, rocking and rolling deliriously in the waves. Suddenly the boat gave a violent lurch; I swung round, pulling out my revolver. I knew what had happened. Behind my back a man had climbed over the side. I fired, thrust him into the water again, watched it turn red. The ship's side loomed steep as a cliff above us, the companion-ladder only reached to my shoulder. Somehow or other, by a colossal effort, I managed to hoist the girl on to the wooden steps, climbed up after her, pushed her up to the deck. We were allowed to stay. No one else came aboard. The ship started moving immediately. It was a triumph.

We traveled on, changing from ship to ship. She could not stand the intense cold, she shivered continually, broke in pieces like a Venetian glass. The disintegration could be observed. She grew thinner and paler, more transparent, ghostlike. It was interesting to watch. She did not move more than was absolutely essential. Her limbs seemed too brittle for use. The seasons ceased to exist, replaced by perpetual cold. Ice walls loomed and thundered, smooth, shining, unearthly, a glacial nightmare; the light of day lost in eerie, iceberg-glittering mirage-light. With one arm I warmed and supported her: the other arm was the executioner's.

The cold abated slightly. We went ashore to wait for a different ship. The country had been at war, the town had suffered severe damage. There was no accommodation available; only one hotel was being rebuilt, only one floor was finished, every habitable room occupied. I could not persuade or bribe anybody to take us in. Travelers were disliked and discouraged: it was natural, in the circumstances. We were told we could stay at some sort of center for strangers outside the town, drove there through the ruined suburbs, everything flattened, no trace of trees or gardens remaining, nothing left standing upright. The country beyond had been a battlefield and was now a desert, covered in shapeless rubbish.

We were deposited at a place which had been a farm. All

around was indescribable chaos. Bits of broken carts, trac-
tors, cars, implements, lay about, bits of old tires, bits of
unrecognizable tools, all mixed up with the debris of shattered weapons and war supplies. Our escort walked cau-
tiously, told us to look out for mines, unexploded bombs.
Inside, the rooms were littered with fragments of all kind of
rubbish, too smashed to identify. They took us to a room
with an earth floor and no furniture, holes in the walls,
roof roughly boarded over, where three people sat on the
ground, propped against the wall. They were silent, unmoving, hardly seemed alive, took no notice when I spoke to
them. I learned later that they were deaf, their eardrums
had burst. There were many in the same state all over the
country, their faces ripped and lips torn by the same deadly
wind. A desperately sick man lay on the floor under a thin
blanket. Great tufts of his hair had fallen out, strips of skin
hung from his hands and face, his loose teeth rattled in
black bleeding gums every time he coughed, he never
stopped coughing and groaning and spitting blood. Emaciated cats wandered in and out, licked the blood with delicate pointed pink tongues.

We had to stop there until the ship came. I longed for
something to focus my eyes on, there was nothing inside or
out; no fields, houses, or roads; only vast quantities of
stones, rubbish, the bones of dead animals. Stones of all
shapes and sizes were spread thick all over the ground to a
depth of two or three feet, often piled up in enormous
mounds, which took the place of hills in a normal landscape. I managed to obtain a horse and rode ten miles
inland, but the awful featureless scene did not change, the
same derelict stony waste extended to the horizon in every
direction, no sign of life or water. The whole country
seemed stone dead, gray in color, no hills except hills of
stones, even its natural contours destroyed by war. The girl
was exhausted, worn out by travel: she did not want to go
on. She kept saying that she must rest, begged me to leave
her and continue the voyage alone. "Don't drag me any

further!" Her voice was fretful. "You only do it to torture me." I replied that I was trying to save her. Anger showed in her eyes. "That's what you say. I was fool enough to believe you the first time." In spite of all attempts to please her, she persisted in treating me as a treacherous enemy. Hitherto I had tried to comfort, to understand. Now her protracted antagonism had its effect, I followed her into the tiny cabin. She struggled, there was no room, the boat rolled, she fell from the berth, her shoulder struck the floor and the soft flesh was hurt. She cried, "You're a brute! A beast! I detest you!" tried to hit me, to struggle up; but I forced her under, forced her to stay down in that hard cold place. She cried out. "I wish I could kill you!" began to sob and struggle hysterically. I slapped the side of her face.

She was afraid of me, but her hostility continued unchanged. Her white, stubborn, frightened child's face got on my nerves. She was still always cold, although the days were gradually getting warmer. She refused my coat. I was obliged to watch her incessant shivering.

She grew emaciated, the flesh seemed to melt off her bones. Her hair lost its glitter, was too heavy, weighed her head down. She kept her head bent, trying not to see me. Listless, she hid in corners or, avoiding me, staggered round the ship, stumbling, her weak legs unable to balance. I no longer felt any desire, gave up talking to her, adopted the warden's silences as my own. I was well aware how sinister my wordless exits and entrances must have seemed, and derived some satisfaction from this.

We were near the end of the journey.

ELEVEN

The gay, undamaged town, full of light and color, freedom, the absence of danger, the warm sun. The faces were happy. The sense of escape brought euphoria. The past was forgotten, the long, hard, dangerous voyage and the preceding nightmare. Nothing but the nightmare had seemed real while it was going on, as if the other lost world had been imagined or dreamed. Now that world, no longer lost, was here the one solid reality. There were theaters, cinemas, restaurants and hotels, shops where goods of all sorts were sold freely, without coupons. The contrast was staggering. The relief overwhelming. The reaction too great. A kind of delirium was induced, a mad gaiety. People sang and danced in the streets, strangers embraced one another. The whole town was decorated as for a festival: flowers everywhere, Chinese lanterns and fairy lights strung from trees, buildings floodlit, elaborate arrangements of colored lights in the parks and gardens. The throb of dance music never stopped. Every night firework displays. All night long fiery stars and rockets burst in the sky, and sank reflected in the dark harbor. The festivities went on and on: carnivals, battles of flowers, balls, regattas, concerts, processions. Nobody wanted to be reminded of what was happening in other parts of the world. Rumors coming from outside were suppressed by order of the consul, who had assumed responsibility for the maintenance of law and order, "pending the restoration of the status quo." To speak of the catastrophe was an offense under the new regulations. The rule was to choose not to know.

Remembering how I myself had wished to forget on another occasion, I understood the euphoric blindness without condoning it. I did not take part in the general rejoicing; I did not feel gay. I had no wish to spend my time dancing or looking at fireworks. Very soon I was utterly sick of bands playing and people in fancy dress. The girl loved all the gaiety, was absolutely transformed by it, her life miraculously renewed. Her weakness and lassitude vanished, she rushed to the shops, bought clothes and cosmetics extravagantly, visited hairdressers, beauty parlors. She seemed a different person. No longer shy, she made friends with people I did not know, drew confidence from their approval, became independent and gay. I scarcely saw anything of her; most of the time I had no idea where she was. She came to me only when she needed money, which I always gave her. For me it was an unsatisfactory situation. I wanted to end it.

I could not remain isolated from the rest of the world. I was involved with the fate of the planet, I had to take an active part in whatever was going on. The endless celebrations here seemed both boring and sinister, reminiscent of the orgies of the plague years. Now, as then, people were deluding themselves; they induced a false sense of security by means of self-indulgence and wishful thinking. I did not believe for one moment they had really escaped.

I observed the weather carefully; it was fine and warm, but not warm enough. I noted particularly how the temperature fell after sunset, producing a definite chill. It was a bad sign. If I mentioned it, I was told this was the cool season. All the same, the sun should have had more power. Looking about, I found other signs of a changing climate. Plants in the tropical gardens were starting to look unhealthy, and I asked a man working there why this was. He gave me a suspicious glance, mumbled an evasive answer: when I persisted, he pretended to hear the head gardener calling, and ran away. I commented on the chilly evenings to some townspeople I saw going about in peculiar wrappings. They were obviously unused to even this mild degree of cold, and possessed no suitable clothing. They too answered evasively and looked at me in alarm. In view of the new regulations, they probably took me for an agent provocateur.

An acquaintance of mine, employed in an official capacity by his government, stopped to refuel his plane. I made contact with him, questioned him about events elsewhere. He was uncommunicative. I understood the reason and did not press him. He could not be certain of my affiliations. Mistakes were not tolerated. An absolute standard of loyalty was demanded. The speaker of an incautious phrase would be eliminated, given no chance to correct an error of judgment. Somewhat reluctantly, he agreed to take me as a passenger when he left, but only as far as another island in the archipelago. I saw on the map that the island inhabited by the Indris was not far away, and, although I had decided to go back to my old profession, I promised myself a short visit to the lemurs before proceeding to the theater of military operations.

I went to inform the girl of my plans. Earlier in the day, waiting to cross a street, I had been held up while a procession went past. She was at its head, standing beside the driver of a big open car decorated with Parma violets. She did not see me, she had no reason to look. Her hair shone like pale fire in the sun, she was smiling and throwing violets to the crowd. It was hard to recognize her as the girl who had traveled with me. When I entered her room, she was still wearing the same Parma violet dress; the delicate color suited her fragile paleness, she looked extremely attractive. Her sparkling hair, sprinkled with silver and Parma violets, had been touched with a matching dye; the slight touch of fantasy was especially charming.

Telling her to open it later, I presented her with a small package containing a bracelet she had admired, and a check on my personal account. "I've brought you some good news, too. I've come to say good-bye." She looked disconcerted, asked what I meant. "I'm leaving tonight. By plane. Aren't you pleased?" As she only stared silently, I went on: "You've always wanted to get rid of me. You must be glad I'm going at last." A pause, then her voice, cold, resentful. "What do you expect me to say?" I was puzzled by this reaction. She continued to survey me coldly, asked with sudden bitterness: "What sort of a man do you think you are?" The tone was meant to be scathing. "Now perhaps you see why I've never trusted you. I always knew you'd betray me again . . . go off and leave me, just as you did before." I protested: "That's grossly unfair! You can't blame me for going after you've told me to go, made it completely clear that you've no time for me—I've hardly set eyes on you since we got here." "Oh . . . !" With a disgusted exclamation, she turned her back, took a few steps away from me.

The full skirt swirling, a silky shimmer like moonlight on violets; the bright, heavy hair swinging, scintillating with violet highlights. I followed, touched her hair with the tips of my fingers, felt it ripple with life. Her arms had a soft satin sheen, the skin smooth and scented, a chain of violets round the thin wrist. I put my arms round her and kissed her neck. Instantly her whole body tensed in violent resistance, she twisted herself away. "Don't touch me! I don't know how you have the nerve . . ." Her voice seemed to fail on the edge of tears, then rose again thinly: "Well, what are you waiting for? Why don't you go? And don't come back this time. I never want to see you again, or be reminded of you!" She pulled off her watch and a ring I had given her, flung them wildly in my direction; began trying to unfasten her necklace, hands at the back of her head, the raised arms giving her slight body a hint of voluptuousness it did not really possess. With an effort I refrained from embracing her again, pleaded with her instead. "Don't be so angry. Don't let's part like this. You must know how I've felt about you all this time. You know how I've always followed you, forced you to come with me. But you've said so consistently that you hated me, wanted nothing to do with me, that I've finally had to believe you." I was only being half honest, and knew it. Tentatively I took her hand; it was stiff, unresponsive, but she did not take it away, let me go on holding it while she gazed at me fixedly. With doubt, criticism, accusation her eyes rested . . . serious, innocent, shadowed eyes; the hand behind her head still engaged with the necklace; the glittering hair, the scent of violets, close to my hand; then the grave voice . . . "And if I hadn't said those things, would you have stayed with me?"

This time it seemed important to speak the whole truth: but I could not be certain what that was, and in the end the only true words seemed to be: "I don't know."

Immediately she became furious, tore her hand out of mine; the other hand tugged at the chain round her neck, broke it, beads shot all over the room. "How can you be so utterly heartless—and so brazen about it! Anyone else would be ashamed . . . but you . . . you don't even pretend to have any feelings . . . it's too horrible, hateful . . . you simply aren't human at all!" I was sorry, I had not wanted to hurt her: I could understand her indignation, in a way. There seemed nothing that I could say. My silence enraged her still more. "Oh, go on! Go away! Go!" She turned on me suddenly, pushed me with a force for which I was unprepared, so that I stumbled back, ran my elbow into the door. It was painful, and I asked in annoyance: "Why are you so anxious to get me out of the room? Are you expecting somebody else? The owner of that open car you were in?" "Oh, how I loathe and despise you! If only you knew how much!" She pushed me again. "Get out, can't you? Go, go, go!" She took a deep breath, lunged at me, started pounding my chest with her fists. But the effort was too much, she abandoned it at once and leaned against the wall, her head drooping. I saw that her shadowed face looked bruised by emotion, before the bright hair swung forward, concealing it. There was a brief pause, long enough for me to feel a chilly sensation creep over me; the adumbration of emptiness, loss . . . of what life would be like without her.

Action was needed to drive away this unpleasant feeling. I put my hand on the door knob, and said, "All right; I'll go now," half hoping to be detained at the last moment. She did not move or speak, made no sign. Only, as I opened the door, a funny little sound escaped from her throat; a sob, a choke, a cough, I could not tell which. I went out into the passage, walked quickly past all the closed doors, back to my own room.

There was still a little time left. I rang for a bottle of Scotch and sat drinking. I felt uncertain, divided in myself. My bag was already packed and had been taken downstairs. In a few minutes I would have to follow . . . unless I changed my plans, stayed here after all . . . I remembered that I had not said good-bye, wondered whether to go back, could not make up my mind. I was still undecided when it was time to go.

I had to pass her door again on the way down. I hesitated outside it for a second, then hurried on to the lift. Of course I was leaving. Only a madman would waste this almost miraculous chance of getting away. I could not possibly hope for another.

TWELVE

The news I heard during the flight confirmed my worst fears. The world situation seemed to be entering its last fatal phase. The elimination of many countries, including my own, left no check on the militarism of the remaining big powers, who confronted each other, the smaller nations dividing allegiance between them. Both principals held stocks of nuclear weapons many times in excess of the overkill stage, so that the balance of terror appeared to be nicely adjusted. But some of the lesser countries also possessed thermonuclear devices, although which of them was not known: and this uncertainty, and the resulting tension, provoked escalating crises, each of which brought nearer the final catastrophe. An insane impatience for death was driving mankind to a second suicide, even before the full effect of the first had been felt. I was profoundly depressed, left with a sense of waiting for something frightful to happen, a sort of mass execution.

I looked at the natural world, and it seemed to share my feelings, to be trying in vain to escape its approaching doom. The waves of the sea sped in disorderly flight toward the horizon; the sea birds, the dolphins and flying fish, hurtled frenziedly through the air; the islands trembled and grew transparent, endeavoring to detach themselves, to rise as vapor and vanish in space. But no escape was possible. The defenseless earth could only lie waiting for its destruction, either by avalanches of ice, or by chain-explosions which would go on and on, eventually transforming it into a nebula, its very substance disintegrated.

I went through the jungle alone, searching for the Indris, believing their magic influence might lift the dead weight of depression which had fallen on me. I did not care whether I saw or dreamed them. It was hot, steamy; the mad intensity of the sun pouring down all its force on the equator for the last time. My head was aching, I was exhausted: unable to stand the burning sun any longer, I lay down in black shade, shut my eyes.

At once I felt that the lemurs were near me. Or *was* it their nearness that abolished despair and dread? It seemed more as if I received a message of hope from another world; a world without violence or cruelty, in which despair was unknown. I had often dreamed of this place, where life was a thousand times more exciting and splendid than life on earth. Now one of its inhabitants seemed to stand beside me. He smiled at me, touched my hand, spoke my name. His face was calm and impartial, tunelessly intelligent, full of goodwill, impossible to associate with any form of pretense.

He told me about the hallucination of space-time, and the joining of past and future so that either could be the present, and all ages accessible. He said he would take me to his world, if I wanted to go. He and others like him had seen the end of our planet, the end of the human race. The race was dying, the collective death-wish, the fatal impulse to self-destruction, although perhaps human life might survive. The life here was over. But life was continuing and expanding in a different place. We could be incorporated in this wider life, if we chose.

I tried to understand. He was a man, but seemed more; he was not what I was. He had access to superior knowledge, to some ultimate truth. He was offering me the freedom of his privileged world, a world my inmost self longed to know. I felt the excitement of the unimaginable experience. From the doomed dying world man had ruined, I seemed to catch sight of this other one, new, infinitely alive, and of boundless potential. For a second I believed myself capable of existing on a higher level in that wonderful world; but saw how far it was beyond my powers when I thought of the girl, the warden, the spreading ice, the fighting and killing. I was part of all that, irrevocably involved with events and persons upon this planet. It was heartbreaking to reject what a part of me wanted most. But I knew that my place was here, in our world under sentence of death, and that I would have to stay and see it through to the end.

The dream, the hallucination, or whatever it was, had a powerful effect on me afterward. I could not forget it, could not forget the supreme intelligence and integrity of that dream-face. I was left with a sense of emptiness, loss, as if something precious really had been in my grasp, and I had thrown it away.

It did not seem to matter what I did now. I was committed to violence and must keep to my pattern. I managed to reach the mainland where guerrilla fighting was going on, and, indifferent to everything, joined a company of mercenaries in the pay of the west. We fought in the marshes, in the delta of a tidal river with many mouths, thigh-deep in mud most of the time. More men had been lost in the mud than through enemy action when finally we were withdrawn. It seemed to me we were fighting against the ice, which was all the while coming steadily nearer, covering more of the world with its dead silence, its awful white peace. By making war we asserted the fact that we were alive and opposed the icy death creeping over the globe.

I still felt I was waiting for something fearful to happen, but in a curious sort of suspended state. There was an emotional blockage. I recognized it in others besides myself. In suppressing food riots, our machine guns indiscriminately cut down rioters and harmless pedestrians. I had no feeling about it and noticed the same indifference in everyone else. People stood looking on as at a performance, did not even attend to the wounded. I had to share a sleeping tent with five other men for a time. They had fantastic courage, but no idea of danger, of life, death, anything; were satisfied as

long as they got a hot meal every day with meat and pota-
toes. I could not make any contact with them; hung up my
overcoat as a screen and lay sleepless behind it.

Presently I began to hear the warden mentioned again.
He was attached to western headquarters, held an important post there. I remembered his wish to cooperate with
the big powers, and admired the way he had achieved it.
Thinking of him made me restless. It seemed idiotic to
spend my last days in a hired fighting unit, and I decided to
ask him to find me a job in which I would have more scope.
The problem was how to reach him. Our leader was the
only person who occasionally had direct dealings with the
higher command, and he refused to help me, interested in
nothing but his own advancement. For days we had been
attacking a strongly defended building said to contain secret
papers. He would not ask for reinforcements, determined to
get the credit for taking the place unaided. By a simple trick,
I enabled him to capture the building and send the documents to headquarters, for which he was highly praised.

Impressed by my ingenuity, he asked me to have a drink
with him, offered me promotion. He was making a personal report the next day, and I said that the only reward I
wanted was to go to headquarters with him. He replied that
he couldn't spare me, I must give him more of these tips. He
was half drunk. I deliberately encouraged him to go on
drinking until he passed out. In the morning, when he was
about to start, I jumped into his car, pretending he had
promised to take me, relying on his having been too drunk
the previous night to remember what had been said. It was
a nasty moment. He clearly suspected something. But he
did not have me thrown out of the car. I drove with him to
headquarters, neither of us speaking a word the whole way.

THIRTEEN

They had built their headquarters far away from the battle-fields, a large clean new building, flying a large clean flag. Stone and concrete, it stood out solid, massive, expensive, indestructible looking, among the low, old, rickety wooden houses. Apart from the sentries at the main entrance, it seemed to have nothing to do with war. No other guards were visible. Inside there appeared to be no security precautions at all. I recalled the commander's drunken remark: perhaps these people really were too soft to fight; relying on their technological supremacy, on the gigantic size and wealth of their country, believed they need not dirty their hands with the actual fighting, paid their inferiors to do that.

I was directed to the warden's suite. The place was air-conditioned. Elevators rose smoothly, silently, swiftly. Thick carpets stretched from wall to wall of the wide corridors. After the squalid discomfort in which I had been living, it was like a luxury hotel. Lights blazed everywhere in spite of the sunshine outside. Windows were hermetically sealed, not made to open. The resulting atmosphere was slightly unreal.

A woman secretary in uniform told me the warden could see no one. He was leaving immediately on a tour of inspection and would be away some days. I said: "I must see him before he goes. It's urgent. I've come all this way specially. I won't keep him a minute." She pursed her lips, shook her head. "Absolutely impossible. He has important papers to sign and gave orders that nobody was to disturb him." Her well made-up face was adamant, uncomprehending. It annoyed me. "To hell with that! I tell you I must see him! It's a personal matter. Can't you understand?" I wanted to shake her, to get some human expression into her face. Instead, I made my voice calm. "At least tell him I'm here and ask whether he'll see me." I felt in my pockets for some means of identification, then wrote my name on a pad. While I was doing so, a colonel came in. The secretary went over and whispered to him. At the end of their confabulation the man said he would give the message himself, took the paper with my name on it, and left the room by the same door through which he had just entered. I knew he had no intention of telling the warden about me. Only decisive action on my part would get me an interview. Soon it would be too late.

"Where does that door lead?" I asked the secretary, pointing to one at the other end of the room. "Oh, that's strictly private. You can't go in there. It's forbidden." For the first time she began to lose her superior calm and to look flustered. She had not been trained to deal with a direct approach. I said: "Well, I'm going in," moved toward the door. "No!" She flew to stand in front of it, barring my way. The country she belonged to was so firmly convinced of world power that its nationals could not conceive of real opposition from anyone, even over the smallest issue. I smiled, pushed her aside. She clung on to my clothes, holding me back. There was a brief scuffle. I heard a voice I recognized beyond the closed door. "What's going on there?" I went in. "Oh, it's you, is it?" He seemed singularly unsurprised. In the doorway the secretary was talking fast and apologetically. He waved her away. The door shut. I said: "I must speak to you."

We were alone in the rich room. Persian rugs on the parquet floor, period furniture, on the wall a full-length portrait of him by a well-known painter. My worn, shabby, unpressed uniform emphasized, by contrast, the elegant grandeur of his, which had gold emblems on cuffs and shoulders, and, on the chest, the ribbons of various orders. He stood up; I had not remembered him as being so tall. The touch of the grand manner he had always had was more marked than when I last saw him. I was not at ease. His presence affected me in the usual way; but, with such obvious differences between us, the idea of contact, however obscure, seemed inappropriate and embarrassing. When he said coldly, "It's no use forcing your way in here. I'm just leaving," I felt confused, and could only repeat: "I must speak to you first." "Impossible. I'm late as it is." He glanced at his watch, started toward the door. "Surely you can wait just a moment!" In my anxiety, I hurriedly stepped in front of him. I should have known better. His eyes flashed; he was angry; I had thrown away my one chance. I cursed myself for a fool. Perhaps my downcast expression amused him: at all events, his attitude suddenly seemed to change, he half smiled. "I can't hold up the entire war just to talk to you. If there's something you *must* say, you'll have to come with me." I was delighted. This was better than anything I had expected. "May I? That's wonderful!" I thanked him enthusiastically. He burst out laughing.

The road to the airfield was lined with people waiting to catch a glimpse of him as we drove past. They stood six deep at the roadside, watched from gardens, windows, balconies, roofs, trees, hoardings, telegraph poles. Some of them must have waited a long time. I was impressed by the force of his immediate impact on the crowd.

Sitting beside him in the plane, I was conscious of curious glances from its other occupants. It was strange to look down and see the earth, not flat or gently curved, but as a segment of a round ball, the sea light blue, the land yellowish-green. Overhead it was dark-blue night. Drinks were brought, I was handed a tinkling glass. "Ice! What luxury!" He glanced at my dilapidated uniform, made a grimace. "You can't expect luxury if you insist on being a hero." The words were mocking, but the smile had some degree of charm. He might even have been taking a friendly interest. "May I ask why you have suddenly become one of our heroic fighters?" I knew I should have spoken about a job. Instead, for some reason, I told him I'd had to do something drastic to cure my depression. "Funny sort of cure. More likely to kill you." "Perhaps that's what I wanted." "No, you're not the suicide type. Anyway, why bother, when we're all going to be killed next week?" "As soon as that?" "Well, perhaps not literally. But certainly very soon." I recognized the trick of blinking his eyes, making the bright blue pupils flash as if they reflected a dazzling blue light. It was the sign that something had not been said. Of course, he had secret information. He always knew everything before anyone else.

An enormous dinner was served. It seemed altogether too lavish, I could not eat half of it. I had got out of the way of eating big meals. Afterward I tried again to say what I had come to say, but the sentences would not take shape in my head. I found myself thinking of him, and remarked on how little surprise he had shown over my arrival. "I was almost expecting you." His expression was rather odd. "You have a way of turning up just before things happen." He seemed to speak quite seriously. "You really expect the catastrophe within weeks or days?" "Looks like it."

Blinds were drawn, shutting out the sky. A film was to be shown. He muttered in my ear: "Wait till their attention's fixed on the screen. Then I'll show you something more interesting. It's supposed to be kept secret." I waited, curious. We left our seats quietly, went through a door, faced an uncovered window. I was confused about time. It had been night overhead all along, but below it was still daylight. There were no clouds. I saw islands scattered over the sea, a normal aerial view. Then something extraordinary, out of this world: a wall of rainbow ice jutting up from the sea, cutting right across, pushing a ridge of water ahead of it as it moved, as if the flat pale surface of sea was a carpet being rolled up. It was a sinister, fascinating sight, which did not seem intended for human eyes. I stared down at it, seeing other things at the same time. The ice world spreading over our world. Mountainous walls of ice surrounding the girl. Her moon-white skin, her hair sparkling with diamond prisms under the moon. The moon's dead eye watching the death of our world.

When we left the plane we were in a remote country, a town I did not know. The warden had come to attend an important conference, people were waiting for him, all sorts of urgent affairs. I was flattered because he seemed in no hurry to leave me. He said: "You should have a look round, it's an interesting place." The town had only lately changed hands, and I asked if the troops had not done a lot of damage; received the reply: "Don't forget some of us are civilized people."

In his splendid uniform he strolled beside me in beautifully kept gardens, attended by armed guards in black and gold. I was proud to be with him. He was a fine-looking man who kept himself in every way at the height of his powers, all his muscles exercised like an athlete's, his intellect and his senses deliberately sharpened. He radiated tremendous dominance, besides an intense physical vitality, zest for living. His aura of power and success seemed to fill the surrounding air, and even extend to me. Walking past artificial cascades, we came to a lily pool where the stream widened. Giant willow trees trailed long green hair in the water, made an inviting grotto of cool green shade. We sat on a stone seat, watched a kingfisher tracing jeweled parabolas. Motionless gray shadows, herons stood here and there in the shallows. It was a private, peaceful, idyllic scene; violence was worlds away. I thought, but did not say, that it seemed a pity people were not allowed to enjoy all this tranquil beauty. As if he read my mind, he told me: "The public used to be admitted on certain days. But we had to suspend the practice on account of vandalism. Hooligans did the damage the armies refrained from doing. There are people you can't teach to appreciate beauty. They're subhuman."

On the far side of the river a troop of small gazelle-like creatures had come to drink, lifting and lowering graceful horned heads. The guards stood at a distance. Alone with my companion, I felt closer to him than ever before; we were like brothers, like identical twin brothers. Drawn to him more strongly than I had ever been, I had to give my feelings some expression, told him how much I appreciated his kindness, how greatly I was honored to be his friend. Something was wrong. He did not smile or acknowledge the compliment, but abruptly stood up. I got up too, while across the water the animals fled, alarmed by our movements. The atmosphere was changing round me; suddenly there was a chill, as if the warm air had passed over ice. I felt a sudden uncomprehended terror, like the sensation that comes in nightmares just before one begins to fall.

In a moment he had turned on me, his eyes flashing blue danger, his face a grim mask. "Where is she?" His voice was fierce, curt, icy. It was as if he had whipped out a gun and pointed it at me. I was horrified; confused by the sudden switch from one emotion to another totally different, I could only stammer stupidly: "I suppose where I left her . . ." He gave me a look of ice. "You mean you don't know?" His accusatory tone froze. I was too appalled to reply.

The guards came closer, formed a circle round us. To shade their eyes, prevent recognition, or inspire dread, they wore as part of their uniform black plastic visors which covered the upper part of the face so that they looked masked. I vaguely remembered hearing about their toughness, that they were convicted thugs and murderers, whose sentences had been remitted in exchange for their absolute loyalty to his person.

"So you've abandoned her." Arrows of blue ice piercing a blizzard, his eyes narrowed and struck. "I hardly expected

that, even of you." The abysmal contempt in his voice made
me wince and mutter: "You know she's always been hostile.
She sent me away." "You don't know how to handle her,"
he stated coldly. "I'd have licked her into shape. She only
needs training. She has to be taught toughness, in life and
in bed." I could not speak, could not collect myself: I was in
a state of shock. When he asked, "What do you propose to
do about her?" I found nothing to say. His eyes were watching me all the time with a frigid scorn and remoteness that
was too painful, too humiliating. Their blue blaze seemed
to stop me thinking. "I shall take her back then." In half a
dozen dry words he disposed of her future, she had no say
in the matter.

At that moment I was more concerned with him, linked
to him so closely, as if we shared the same blood. I could
not bear to be alienated from him. "Why are you so angry?"
I went a step closer, tried to touch his sleeve, but he moved
out of my reach. "Is it only because of her?" I could not
believe this, the bond between him and myself seemed so
strong. Just then she was nothing to me by comparison, not
even real. We could have shared her between us. I may have
said something of the kind. His face was carved in stone,
his cold voice hard enough to cut steel, he was thousands of
miles away. "As soon as I can make time I shall go and fetch
her. And then keep her with me. You won't see her again."

There was no bond, never had been, except in my imagination. He was not my friend, had never been close to me,
identification was nothing but an illusion. He was treating
me as someone beneath contempt. In a feeble attempt to
re-establish myself, I said I had tried to save her. His eyes
were terribly hard and blue, I could hardly meet them. His
face was a statue's, stony, it did not change. I forced myself
to go on looking him in the face. Only his mouth finally
moved to say: "She will be saved, if that's possible. But not
by you." Then he turned and strolled off in his grand uniform with gold epaulets. A few paces away he paused, lit a

cigarette, keeping his back toward me, strolled on again without giving me a glance. I saw him lift one hand and make a sign to the guards.

They closed in, inhuman in their black masks. Rubber truncheons crashed into me, I was kicked in the groin, in falling my head must have struck the stone seat, I passed out. This was lucky for me. Apparently it did not amuse them to beat an unconscious body. There was no sign of them when I came round. My head throbbed and rang, even to open my eyes was a fearful effort, every inch of my body ached, but nothing was broken. Pain confused me, made me uncertain of what had happened, of the length of time that had elapsed, of the sequence of events. In my confusion I could not understand being let off so lightly, until it occurred to me that the guards meant to come back later to finish the job. If they found me here I was done for. I could hardly move, but with infinite labor dragged myself down to the river, everything swaying round me, fell among rushes and lay for some time with my face in the mud.

When a far-off sound roused me it was almost dark. In the distance a semicircle of dark shapes was slowly advancing, as if searching. I got a fright, I thought they were people looking for me and kept quite motionless. They must have been animals grazing, for when I next looked up they had gone. The shock made me realize that I had to get moving. I crawled on to the water's edge, let the river run over the wound in my head, washed another deep gash on my cheekbone, washed off some of the blood and mud.

The cold water revived me. Somehow or other I managed to reach the park gates, even started walking along a street, but collapsed after a short distance. A carload of noisy young people coming back from a celebration saw me lying in the road and stopped to investigate. They thought I was one of their party who had fallen down drunk. I persuaded them to drive me to the hospital, where a doctor attended to me. I invented some story to account for my injuries and was given a bed in the casualty department. I slept for two or three hours. The clanging bell of an ambulance woke me. Stretcherbearers came tramping in. To move was appallingly difficult, all I wanted was to lie still and go on sleeping. But I knew it was too dangerous, I dared not stay any longer.

While the night staff were occupied with the new arrival, I crept through a side door into a dark corridor and left the building.

FOURTEEN

My head was aching, everything was confused inside it. I knew only that I had to get out of the town before daylight. I could not think. The hallucination of one moment did not fit the reality of the next. In a narrow alley, a car came tearing toward me to run me down, filling the whole space between alp-high houses. With bleeding knuckles I staggered from door to locked door, at the last moment crushed myself up against one. In uniform, immensely grand, the warden drove past in his great black car. The girl was with him, her hair shimmering violet like the shadows of trees on snow. They drove through the snow together under a white fur rug, wide as a room, deep as a snowdrift, edged with cabochon rubies.

Lit by the dazzling cold fire of the aurora borealis, they walked among glittering icebergs; a blizzard blew arctic white, his bone-white forehead and icicle eyes, her silver-frosted hair bright with ice flowers under the pole star. A thunderclap boomed in the ice. He fought a polar bear, strangled it with his hands, to train her in toughness taught her to take the skin with his wicked knife. When it was done, she crept close for warmth. The huge skin covered them both, its long white hairs tipped with blood. The snowy thickness hid their two bodies; blood dripping from the tips of the dense fur turned the snow blood-red.

I saw her standing in torchlight with dreaming eyes. I watched her, wanted her, wanted to take her away with me. But that other had claimed her; her white girl's body fell through the smoke of smoldering torches across his knees. I was out searching for her, marauders were sacking the town. I searched everywhere, could not find her, stumbled over her in the rubble, her head awry. Through the smoke and dust filling the air, I saw her skin white against dirt and debris, the blood first red and then black on the white, her head twisted sideways by the unbelievable hair, the slender neck broken. Victimization in childhood had made her accept the fate of a victim, and whatever I did or did not do this fate would ultimately achieve itself. To leave her to it was one thing. To leave her to that man was quite a different thing. It was something I could not do.

I had to get to her before he did. But the difficulties were overwhelming. The total absence of transport meant resorting to bribery, every kind of deception, worse. In my mind's eye I kept seeing the iceline moving across the ocean, toward the islands, toward that particular island I had not identified on the map. I thought of her at the center, not knowing she was encircled, while we advanced toward her from different sides, I from one point, he from another, and then the ice . . . My chances of arriving first seemed almost nonexistent. Every mile would be slow and difficult for me. He could get to her by plane in just a few hours, whenever he felt inclined. I could only hope for the important conference he was now attending and other military matters to detain him as long as possible. But I was not optimistic.

My head wound and slashed face had begun to heal normally, but I did not feel normal. My head ached all the time, I was pursued by horrific visions, disasters exploding in violent death, universal destruction. I was always aware that I was going to execution. Not that my own death seemed to matter. I had lived, I had done things, I had seen the world. I did not want to grow old, deteriorate, lose my intelligence and my physical faculties. But I had this compulsive urge to see the girl once more; to be the first to reach her.

I had to travel an enormous distance. Because I could not risk crossing the frontier openly, for two days I went on foot through wild country, without shelter, without food or drink. Later I had the luck to be taken some of the way by helicopter. A naked woman, life-size, was painted on the side in crude colors; pop art in the midst of war. A person in occupation had to be disposed of; I was not going to lose the chance of a lift. The luck did not last. In a frenzy I searched the wreckage for the man who had been shot down. Only the painted face simpered at me among the debris, round pink circles for cheeks, black eyes blankly serene as a painted doll's.

In a country at war I tried to keep away from the fighting, came to a town unexpectedly quiet, except for the lorries that thundered through, crammed with troops or workers. A dull gray day and a dull gray town, sickly women languidly slapping their dirty washing on flat river stones. I was worn out and started to lose heart. Without some form of transport I would never complete my journey. I saw nothing encouraging here. Passers-by averted their eyes when I looked at them; they were suspicious of strangers, and with my scarred face, my old torn muddy guerrilla's outfit, my appearance could not have been reassuring. I went about searching for someone who looked approachable, found no such person. I talked to the owner of a garage, offered him money, a new foreign rifle with telescopic sights; he threatened to call the police, would do nothing to help me.

At dusk it began to rain, rained harder as night came on. A curfew was in force: no light showed from the houses, the streets were empty. I was taking a risk by staying outside, but was too despondent to care. A siren howled, distant crashes, gradually coming nearer, followed at intervals, alternating with bursts of gunfire. Rain fell in sheets, the street had become a river. I sheltered under an archway, shivered, could not think what to do; my brain seemed paralyzed by discomfort. I felt desperate, in despair.

A big military car swished past, stopped on the opposite side of the road. Impregnable in steel helmet, overcoat and high boots, the driver got out and went into a house. The desultory bombardment was still going on. There was no need for silence. In desperation, I prized up one of the granite cobbles, hurled it through a ground-floor window, put my hand in, pushed up the glass, swung myself over the sill. Before my feet touched the floor, the door of the room opened, I faced the man from the car. A sudden much louder explosion rocked everything, filled the dark room with a fiery blaze, reflected on cheekbones, eyeballs. Blood gushed from the wound, ran in dark rivers I tried to check, while I dragged off his uniform, put it on, forced him into my tattered clothes. By good luck we were about the same size. I went round hurriedly, wrecking the room, threw the furniture about, smashed mirrors, opened drawers, ripped pictures with my knife, to make it look as if a looter had broken in and been shot by the householder. I could not stand the weight of the metal helmet on my head. Carrying it in my hand, I went out, dressed as the other man, got into the armored car, drove away. I had not succeeded in keeping his blood off the uniform, but with the fur-lined coat fastened the stains did not show.

I was stopped at a checkpoint on the outskirts. A bomb obligingly dropped near by. There was chaos, the guards had no time to interrogate me. I bluffed my way through and drove on. I knew I had not satisfied them, that they suspected something; but I thought they were too busy to worry about me. I was wrong. I had only gone a few miles when searchlights spotlit the car, I heard the roar of supercharged motorcycles behind me. One rider hurtled past, ordering me to stop. Just ahead, he braked hard, stayed straddled in the middle of the road, suicidal, his gun pointed at me, spitting bullets which bounced off like hailstones. I put on speed, hit him squarely, glanced back, saw a black shape fly over handlebars and another crash down, as the next two machines skidded into the wreck and piled up. The shooting went on for a bit, but no one came after me. I hoped the survivors would stay to clean up the mess and give me time to get right away. The rain stopped, warlike noises died out, I began to relax. Then my headlights caught figures in uniform hurrying off the road, patrol cars blocking it, parked right across. Somebody must have telephoned on ahead. I wondered why they thought me important enough to send out all these people; decided they must already have found the man who should have been driving, and that the importance was his. They started firing. I accelerated, vaguely recalling the warden's story of crashing a frontier barrier, as the car burst through the obstruction like tissue paper. More shots followed harmlessly. Soon all was quiet, I had the road to myself, no further sign of pursuit. When I crossed the border half an hour afterward, I knew I was clear at last.

The chase had a bracing effect on me. Single-handed I had defeated the organized force which had been used against me. I was stimulated, as if I had won a fast and exciting game. At last I felt normal again, my old self, no longer a despairing traveler in need of help, but strong, independent, powerful. The mechanical power I controlled had become my own. I stopped to examine the car. Except for a few dents and scratches it was none the worse. The tank was still three-quarters full, the back packed with numerous cans of petrol, far more than I needed to get to my destination. I discovered a large package of food: biscuits, cheese, eggs, chocolate, apples, a bottle of rum. I should not have to bother about stopping to get supplies.

Suddenly I was on the last lap of the journey. In spite of difficulties which had seemed insurmountable, my objective was almost in sight. I was pleased with my achievement, and with myself. I did not think about the killing involved. If I had acted differently I should never have got here. In any case, the hour of death had only been anticipated slightly, every living creature would soon perish. The whole world was turning toward death. Already the ice had buried millions; the survivors distracted themselves with fighting and rushing about, but always knew the invincible enemy was advancing, and that wherever they went, the ice would be there, the conqueror, in the end. The only thing was to extract what satisfaction one could from each moment. I enjoyed rushing through the night in the high-powered car, exhilarated by the speed and my own skillful driving, by the feeling of excitement and danger. When I got tired I pulled up at the roadside, slept for an hour or so.

The cold woke me at dawn. All night long freezing stars had bombarded the earth with ice-rays, which penetrated its surface and were stored beneath, leaving only a thin crust over a reservoir of ice cold. In this sub-tropical region, to see the ground white with rime and feel it frozen hard underfoot gave the impression of having stepped out of everyday life, into a field of strangeness where no known laws operated. I ate a quick breakfast, put the engine in gear, and sped toward the horizon, toward the sea. On a good road, I drove fast, at ninety miles an hour, flying over the desolate land, at long intervals passing the remains of a house or a village. Although I never saw anyone, I could feel eyes watching me from the ruins. People saw the army car and kept quiet, did not reveal themselves; they had learned that it was safer to remain hidden.

The day got colder as it went on, the sky darkened. Rising beyond the mountains behind me, ominous masses of black cloud were converging upon the sea. I watched these clouds, understood their meaning; felt the intensifying cold with increasing dread. I knew it meant only one thing: the glaciers were closing in. Instead of my world, there would soon be only ice, snow, stillness, death; no more violence, no war, no victims; nothing but frozen silence, absence of life. The ultimate achievement of mankind would be, not just self-destruction, but the destruction of all life; the transformation of the living world into a dead planet.

In a sky which should have been cloudless and burning blue, the somber, enormous structures of storm cloud looked inexpressibly sinister, threatening, like monstrous ruins on the point of collapse, hanging impossibly overhead. Icy crystalline shapes began to flower on the windscreen. I was oppressed by the sense of universal strangeness, by the chill of approaching catastrophe, the menace of ruins suspended above; and also by the enormity of what had been done, the weight of collective guilt. A frightful crime had been committed, against nature, against the universe, against life. By rejecting life, man had destroyed the immemorial order, destroyed the world; now everything was about to crash down in ruins.

A gull flew close and cried; I had reached the sea. I sniffed the salt smell, looked over the dark waves to the horizon, saw no wall of ice. But the air was full of the deadly coldness of ice, it could not be far away. I raced across fifty miles of bare land to the town. Above it, the clouds hung lower, blacker, more ominous, waiting for me to arrive. The cold made me shiver: perhaps *he* had already been there. When I slowed down and entered the streets where people had danced all night, I could hardly believe this was the same gay place. The streets were all deserted and silent; no pedestrians, no traffic, no flowers, no music, no lights. I saw sunken ships in the harbor; demolished buildings, closed shops and hotels; a cold gray light that belonged to another climate, a different part of the world; everywhere the imminent threat of a new ice age.

I saw what was in front of my eyes, and at the same time I saw the girl. Her picture was always with me, in my wallet and in my head. Now her image appeared in the open wherever I looked. Her white lost face was everywhere with its too-large eyes, her albino paleness flared like a torch beneath the malignant clouds, drew my eyes like a magnet. She was a shimmer among the ruins, her hair a glittering in the dark day. Her wide eyes of a wronged and terrified child accused me from the black holes of smashed windows. Like a perverted child she ran past, soliciting me with big eyes, tempting me with the pleasure of watching her pain, elaborating the worst imaginings of my desire. The ghostly gleam of her face lured me into the shadows, her hair was a cloud of light; but as I came near her she turned and fled, the silver shifting suddenly on her shoulders, a waterfall glinting in moonlight.

The remains of a roadblock obstructed the entrance to the hotel at which we had stayed. I had to leave the car and walk up the drive. A strong wind, cruelly cold, blew straight off the ice, tore my breath away. I kept glancing at the anthracite-colored sea to make sure the ice itself was not already in sight. At ground level the exterior of the hotel was unchanged, but higher up the walls were full of great gaping holes, the roof sagged. I went inside. It was cold and dark, no heating, no light, dilapidated chairs and tables arranged as in a café. In spite of fragments of gilt decoration surviving amidst the destruction, I did not recognize the wrecked room.

I heard uneven steps, the tap of a stick, was approached by someone who knew my name. The young man's appearance was vaguely familiar, but at first I could not place him in the dim light. Suddenly it came back to me while we were shaking hands. "Of course, you're the proprietor's son." The lameness was new and had put me off. He nodded. "My parents are dead. Killed in the bombing. Officially I'm dead too." I asked what had happened. He grimaced, touched his leg. "It was in the retreat. All the wounded were left behind. When I heard I'd been reported killed I didn't bother to contradict . . ." He broke off, gave me a nervous glance. "But what on earth brings you back? You can't stay here, you know. We're in the area of immediate danger. Everyone's been told to get out. There are only a few of us old inhabitants left."

I looked at him; did not understand why he was uneasy with me. He told me the crowds of people I had seen here had left long ago. "They almost all got away before war broke out." I said I had come in the hope of finding the girl. "But I ought to have realized that she would have gone." I waited for him to say something about the warden. Instead, he looked awkward, hesitated before he spoke. "As a matter of fact, she's one of the very few who did *not* go." My emotions had been disturbed during the last few seconds; to disguise the fact as much as to make sure my present relief was justified, I asked if any inquiries had been made about her. "No." He looked blank, seemed to be speaking the truth. "Does she still live here?" Again the reply was "No." He went on: "We've been using this part as a restaurant, but the whole building's unsafe. There's nobody left to do repair work. Anyhow, what's the use?" I agreed that the approach of the ice made all such activities futile. But I was only interested in the girl. "Where is she living now?" His hesitation was longer this time, more marked. He was obviously embarrassed by the question, and when he finally answered it, I at once saw why. "Quite near. At the beach house." I stared at him. "I see." Everything was clear now. I remembered the house well, it was his home, where he had lived with his parents. He continued uncomfortably: "It's convenient for her. She's been doing some work here." "Really? What sort of work?" I was curious. "Oh, helping in the restaurant." He sounded evasive, vague. "Do you mean waiting on people?" "Well, she sometimes dances . . ." As if to avoid the topic, he said: "It's a great pity she didn't go to a safe place like everyone else, while it was still possible. She had friends who would have taken her with them." I replied: "Evidently she had friends here she preferred to stay with." I watched him closely, but his face was in shadow, his back to the fading light, I could not make out his expression.

All at once I became impatient. I had already wasted too much time on him. She was the one I had to talk to. On my way to the door I asked: "Have you any idea where I'd be likely to find her?" "I should think she'd be in her room. She's not due here till later." He limped after me, leaning on the stick. "I'll show you a short cut through the garden." I got the impression he was trying to delay me. "Many thanks: but I can find my own way." I opened the door and went out; shut it between us before he had time to say anything more.

FIFTEEN

An ice-cold air-stream hit me outside. Dusk was falling, the wind brought crumblings of frozen snow. I did not look for the short cut, but took a path I knew led down to the beach. Frost had killed off the exotic plants I remembered growing beside it: the leaves of palm trees were shriveled, moribund, blackened, furled tight like rolled umbrellas. I should have been inured to climatic changes; but I again felt I had moved out of ordinary life into an area of total strangeness. All this was real, it was really happening, but with a quality of the unreal; it was reality happening in quite a different way.

Snow began to fall steadily, driven into my face by the arctic wind. The cold scorched my skin, froze my breath. To keep the snow out of my eyes I put on the heavy helmet. By the time the beach came in sight, a thick crust of ice had formed on the brim, making it still heavier. Through the white shifting curtain the house dimly appeared ahead; but I could not make out whether waves or a huge uneven expanse of pack ice lay beyond. It was heavy going against the wind. The snow thickened, inexhaustibly falling, incessantly sifting down, spreading a sheet of sterile whiteness over the face of the dying world, burying the violent and their victims together in a mass grave, obliterating the last trace of man and his works.

Suddenly, through the churning white, I saw the girl running away from me, toward the ice. I tried to shout, "Stop! Come back!" but the polar air corroded my throat, my voice was whirled away by the wind. Snow powder blowing round me like mist, I ran after her. I could hardly see her, hardly see out of my eyes: I had to pause, painfully wipe away the crystals of ice forming on my eyeballs, before I could continue. The murderous wind kept hurling me back, the snow heaped up white hills that fumed like volcanoes, blinding me again with white smoke. In the awful dead cold I lurched on, staggered and stumbled, slipped, fell, struggled up, reached her somehow at last, clutched her with numbed hands.

I was too late, I saw at once that we had no chance. A mirage-like arctic splendor towered all around, a weird, unearthly architecture of ice. Huge ice-battlements, rainbow turrets and pinnacles, filled the sky, lit from within by frigid mineral fires. We were trapped by those encircling walls, a ring of ghostly executioners, advancing slowly, inexorably, to destroy us. I could not move, could not think. The executioner's breath paralyzed, dulled the brain. I felt the fatal chill of the ice touch me, heard its thunder, saw it split by dazzling emerald fissures. Far overhead the iceberg-glittering heights boomed and shuddered, about to fall. Frost glimmered on her shoulders, her face was ice-white, the long eyelashes swept her cheek. I held her close, clasped her tightly against my chest, so that she should not see the mountainous masses of falling ice.

In her gray loden coat, she stood on the verandah surrounding the beach house, waiting for someone. At first I thought she had seen me coming, then realized that her eyes were fixed on a different path. I stopped and stood watching. I wanted to make sure who it was she expected, although I did not think the hotel man was likely to come now, knowing I would be here. She seemed to feel she was no longer alone, started looking about, and finally saw me. I was not close enough to distinguish the dilating pupils that made her eyes huge and black in her white face. But I heard her sharp exclamation, saw the hair swirl and glint as she swung round, pulled the hood over her head, and started toward the beach. I could hardly see her once she was off the verandah. She was trying to become invisible in the snow. Sudden terror had seized her: the thought of the man whose ice-blue eyes had a magnetic power which could deprive her of will and thrust her down into hallucination and horror. The fear she lived with, always near her, close behind the world's normal façade, had become concentrated on him. And there was another connected with him, they were in league together, or perhaps they were the same person.

Both of them persecuted her, she did not understand why. But she accepted the fact as she accepted all the things that happened to her, expecting to be ill-treated, to be made a victim, ultimately to be destroyed, either by unknown forces or by human beings. This fate seemed always to have been waiting for her, ever since time began. Only love might have saved her from it. But she had never looked for love. Her part was to suffer; that was known and accepted. Fatality brought resignation. It was no use fighting against her fate. She knew she had been beaten before the start.

She had gone only a few steps when I overtook her and pulled her back to the shelter of the verandah. Wiping the snow off her face, she exclaimed, "Oh, it's you," stared at me in surprise. "Who did you think it was?" I remembered the uniform I was wearing. "These clothes aren't mine, by the way. I borrowed them." Her apprehension vanished, she showed relief, her manner became quite different, suddenly she seemed self-possessed. I was familiar with the air of confidence and independence she could assume when people or circumstances made her feel secure. The young man at the hotel must have done this. "Let's go in quickly. Why are we standing here?" She spoke casually, acted as though my return had been planned and expected, pretending there was nothing unusual about the situation. It was annoying, after all I had been through. I knew it was meant to make me feel small.

She led the way to her door, invited me in with a social gesture. The little room was bare and cold, an old-fashioned oil heater barely took off the chill. But everything was clean and tidy, I saw that affectionate care had been expended, there were decorations of driftwood and shells from the beach. "I'm afraid it's not very comfortable; not up to your standard." She was trying to make fun of me. I said nothing. She undid her coat and put back the hood, shaking her hair free. It had grown longer, sparkled and shimmered with life. Under the coat she was wearing an expensive-looking gray suit I had not seen, which had evidently been made to measure. So she had not been short of money. To see her looking attractive and well dressed for some reason added to my annoyance.

Like a conventional hostess making conversation, she said: "It's nice to have a place of one's own after so much traveling about." I stared at her. I had come so far to find her, through so many deaths and dangers and difficulties: now at last I had reached her; and she was talking to me like a stranger. It was too much. I felt hurt and resentful. Exasperated by her offhand pose and her determination to deprive my arrival of its importance, I said indignantly: "Why are you putting on this act? I didn't come all this way just to be treated as a casual caller."

"Did you expect me to put out the red carpet for you?" The feeble flippant retort sounded offensive. I was becoming angry, knew I would not be able to control myself much longer. When, still keeping up the farce, she inquired in the same artificial tone what I had been doing, I answered coldly: "I've been with someone you know," giving her a long, hard, meaning look at the same time. She understood at once, dropped her affectations and showed signs of anxiety. "When I first saw you . . . I thought you . . . he . . . I was afraid he'd arrived here." "He will be here at any moment. I came to tell you that. To warn you, in case you have other plans, that he means to get you back—" She interrupted, "No, no—never!" shaking her head so vigorously that the hair flew out with a sheen like spray. I said: "Then you must leave immediately. Before he comes."

"Leave here?" It was cruel. She looked round in dismay at the home she had made. The sea shells comforted, the little room was so reassuring, so safe, the one place on earth she could call her own. "But why? He'll never find me . . ." Her wistful, pleading voice did not touch me; mine remained adamant, cold. "Why not? *I* found you." "Yes, but you knew . . ." She looked at me with suspicion, I was not to be trusted. "You didn't tell him, did you?" "Of course not. I want you to come with *me*."

All of a sudden her confidence was restored, she reverted to her former disparaging attitude, gave me a derisive glance. "With *you*? Oh, no! Surely we haven't got to go through all *that* again!" Attempting sarcasm, she rolled her big eyes, turned them up to the ceiling. It was a deliberate insult. I was outraged. Her slighting tone belittled my desperate efforts to reach her, ridiculed everything I had endured. In a furious rage suddenly, I took hold of her roughly, gave her a violent shake. "Stop it, will you! I can't stand any more! Stop being so damned insulting! I've just been through hell for your sake, traveled hundreds of miles under ghastly conditions, run fantastic risks, almost got myself killed. And not the slightest sign of appreciation from you . . . not one word of thanks at the end of it . . . you don't even treat me with ordinary common politeness . . . I only get a cheap sneer . . . Charming gratitude! Charming way to behave!" She was gazing at me speechlessly, her eyes all black pupil. My rage did not become any less. "Even now you haven't got the decency to apologize!"

Still infuriated, I went on abusing her, called her insufferable, impertinent, insolent, vulgar. "In future you might at least be civil enough to thank people who do things for you, instead of displaying your stupid conceited rudeness by laughing at them!" She seemed stricken, dumb; stood before me in silence, with hanging head, all trace of assurance gone. In the last few moments she had become a withdrawn, frightened, unhappy child, damaged by adult deviations.

A pulse at the base of her neck caught my eye, beating rapidly like something under the skin trying to escape. I had noticed it on other occasions when she was frightened. It had its usual effect on me now. I said loudly: "What a fool I've been to worry about you. I suppose you moved in with your boyfriend as soon as I left." She looked up at me quickly, apprehensively, stammered: "What do you mean?" "Oh, don't pretend you don't understand—it's too sickening!" My voice sounded aggressive, got louder and louder. "I mean the owner of this house, of course. The fellow you're living with. The one you were waiting for on the verandah when I arrived." I could hear myself shouting. The noise terrified her. She had begun to tremble, her mouth was shaking. "I was *not* waiting for him—" She saw what I was doing, broke off. "Don't lock the door . . ." I had locked it already. Everything had turned to iron, to ice, to hard, cold, burning impatience. I grasped her shoulders, pulled her toward me. She resisted, cried, "Keep away from me!" kicked, struggled, her hand shot out, dislodging a bowl of delicate wing-shaped shells, which smashed on the floor: our feet ground them to rainbow powder. I forced her down, crushed her under the bloodstained tunic, the sharp buckle of the uniform belt caught her arm. Blood beading the soft white flesh . . . the iron taste of blood in my mouth . . .

She lay silent, unmoving, avoiding me by turning her face to the wall. Perhaps because I could not see her face, she seemed like someone I did not know. I felt nothing whatever about her, all feeling had left me. I had said I could not stand any more, and that was the truth. I could not go on; it was all too humiliating, too painful. I had wanted to finish with her in the past, but had been unable to do so. Now the moment had come. It was time to get up and go, to end the whole wretched business. I had let it go on far too long, it had always been painful and unrewarding. She did not move when I stood up. Neither of us said a word. We were like two strangers accidentally in the same room. I was not thinking. All I wanted was to get into the car and drive and drive, until I was somewhere far away where I could forget all this. I left the room without looking at her or speaking, and went out into the arctic cold.

Outside it had got quite dark. I paused on the verandah for my eyes to get used to the blackness. By degrees the snow became visible as it fell, a sort of faint shimmer like phosphorescence. The hollow roar of the wind came in irregular bursts, the snowflakes whirled madly in all directions, filled the night with their spectral chaos. I seemed to feel the same feverish disorder in myself, in all my pointless rushing from place to place. The crazily dancing snowflakes represented the whole of life. Her image flew past, the silver hair streaming, and was instantly swept away in the wild confusion. In the delirium of the dance, it was impossible to distinguish between the violent and the victims. Anyway, distinctions no longer mattered in a dance of death, where all the dancers spun on the edge of nothing.

I had grown used to the feeling that I was going toward execution. It was something in the distance, an idea with which I had become familiar. Now it suddenly sprang at me, stood close at my elbow, no longer an idea, but a reality, just about to happen. It gave me a shock, a physical sensation in the pit of the stomach. The past had vanished and become nothing; the future was the inconceivable nothingness of annihilation. All that was left was the ceaselessly shrinking fragment of time called "now."

I remembered the dark-blue sky of noon and midnight which I had seen above, while below a wall of rainbow ice moved over the ocean, round the globe. Pale cliffs looming, radiating dead cold, ghostly avengers coming to end mankind. I knew the ice was closing in round us, my own eyes had seen the ominous moving wall. I knew it was coming closer each moment, and would go on advancing until all life was extinct.

I thought of the girl I had left in the room behind me, a child, immature, a glass girl. She had not seen, did not understand. She knew she was doomed, but not the nature of her fate, or how to face it. No one had ever taught her to stand alone. The hotel proprietor's son had not impressed me as particularly reliable or protective, but rather a weak

unsatisfactory type, and disabled as well. I did not trust
him to look after her when the crisis came. I saw her,
defenseless and terrified, amidst the collapsing mountains
of ice; above the crashes and thunder, heard her feeble
pathetic cries. Knowing what I knew, I could not leave her
alone and helpless. She would suffer too much.

I went back indoors. She did not seem to have moved, and
although she looked round when I came into the room, at
once twisted away again. She was crying and did not want
me to see her face. I went close to the bed, stood there without touching her. She looked pathetic, cold, shivering, her
skin had the same faint mauve tinge as some of the shells. It
was too easy to hurt her. I said quietly: "I must ask you something. I don't care how many different men you've slept
with—it's not about that. But I must know why you were so
insulting to me just now. Why have you been trying to humil-
iate me ever since I arrived?" She would not look round, I
thought she was not going to answer; but then, with long
gaps between the words, she brought out: "I wanted . . . to
get . . . my . . . own . . . back . . ." I protested: "But what for?
I'd only just got here. I hadn't done anything to you."

"I knew . . ." I had to bend over her to catch the accusing
voice, speaking through tears. "Whenever I see you, I
always know you'll torment me . . . kick me around . . .
treat me like some sort of slave . . . if not at once, in an hour
or two, or next day . . . you're sure to . . . you always do . . ."
I was startled, almost shocked. The words presented a view
of myself I much preferred not to see. I hurriedly asked her
another question. "Who *were* you waiting for on the verandah, if it wasn't the hotel fellow?" Once more a totally
unexpected answer disconcerted me. "For you . . . I heard
the car . . . I thought . . . I wondered . . ." This time I was
astounded, incredulous. "But that can't possibly be true—
not after what you've just said. Besides, you didn't know I
was coming. I don't believe it."

She twisted round wildly, sat up, flung back the mass of
pale hair, showed her desolate victim's face, features dis-

solved in tears, eyes black as if set in bruises. "It *is* true, I tell you, whether you believe it or not! I don't know why . . . you're always so horrible to me . . . I only know I've always waited . . . wondered if you'd come back. You never sent any message . . . but I always waited for you . . . stayed here when the others left so that you'd be able to find me . . ." She looked a desperate child, sobbing out the truth. But what she said was so incredible that I said again: "It's not possible—it can't be true." Face convulsed, she gasped in a voice choked by tears: "Haven't you had enough yet? Can't you *ever* stop bullying me?"

Suddenly I felt ashamed, muttered: "I'm sorry . . ." I wished I could somehow obliterate past words and actions. She had thrown herself down again, flat on her face. I stood looking at her, not knowing what to say. The situation seemed to have gone beyond words. In the end I could think of nothing better than: "I didn't come back only to ask those questions, you know." There was no response at all. I was not even sure she had heard me. I stood waiting, while the sobs slowly died away. In the silence, I watched the pulse in her neck, still beating fast, presently put out my hand, gently touched the spot with the tip of one finger, then let the hand fall. A skin like white satin, hair the color of moonlight . . .

Slowly she turned her head toward me without a word; her mouth appeared out of the shining hair, then her wet brilliant eyes, glittering between long lashes. Now she had stopped crying; but at intervals a shudder, a soundless gasp, interrupted her breathing, like an interior sob. She did not say anything. I waited. The seconds passed. When I could not wait any longer, I asked softly: "Are you coming with me? I promise I won't bully you any more." She did not answer, so after a moment I was obliged to add: "Or do you want me to go?" Abruptly she sat up straight, made a distraught movement, but still did not speak. I waited again: tentatively held out my hands; lived through another long silence, interminable suspense. At last she gave me her hands. I kissed them, kissed her hair, lifted her off the bed.

While she was getting ready I stood at the window, staring out at the snow. I was wondering whether I ought to tell her that I had seen the sinister ice-wall approaching across the sea, and that in the end it was bound to destroy us and everything else. But my thoughts were muddled and inconclusive and I reached no decision.

She said she was ready, and went to the door; stopped there, looking back at the room. I saw her psychologically bruised face, her extreme vulnerability, her unspoken fears. This little room the one friendly familiar place. Everything outside terrifyingly strange. The huge alien night, the snow, the destroying cold, the menacing unknown future. Her eyes turned to me, searched my face: a heavy, doubting, reproachful look, accusing and questioning at the same time. I was another very disturbing factor; she had absolutely no reason to trust me. I smiled at her, touched her hand. Her lips moved slightly in what, in different circumstances, might have become a smile.

We went out together into the onslaught of snow, fled through the swirling white like escaping ghosts. With no light but the snow's faint phosphorescent gleam, it was hard to keep to the path. Even with the wind behind us, walking was hard labor. The distance to the car seemed much greater than I had thought. I held her arm to guide her and help her along. When she stumbled I put my arm round her, steadied her, held her up. Under the thick loden coat she was cold as ice, her hands felt frozen through my heavy gloves. I tried to rub some warmth into them, for a moment she leaned on me, her face a moonstone, luminous in the dark, her lashes tipped white with snow. She was tired, I sensed the effort she made to start walking again. I encouraged her, praised her, kept my arm round her waist, picked her up and carried her the last part of the way.

When we were in the car, I switched on the heater before doing anything else. The interior was warm in less than a minute, but she did not relax, sat beside me silent and tense. Catching a sidelong suspicious glance, I felt myself justly accused. After the way I had treated her, suspicion was all I deserved. She could not know that I had just discovered a new pleasure in tenderness. I asked if she was hungry; she shook her head. I produced some chocolate from the food parcel, offered it to her. No chocolate had been available for civilians for a very long time. I remembered she used to like this particular brand. She looked at it doubtfully, seemed about to refuse, then relaxed suddenly, took it, thanked me with a timid and touching smile. I wondered why I had waited so long to be kind to her, until it was almost too late. I said nothing about our ultimate fate, or about the ice-wall coming nearer and nearer. Instead, I told her the ice would stop moving before it reached the equator; that we would find a place there where we would be safe. I did not think this was remotely possible, did not know whether she believed it. However the end came, we should be together; I could at least make it quick and easy for her.

Driving the big car through the glacial night I was almost happy. I did not regret that other world I had longed for and lost. My world was now ending in snow and ice, there was nothing else left. Human life was over, the astronauts underground, buried by tons of ice, the scientists wiped out by their own disaster. I felt exhilarated because we two were alive, racing through the blizzard together.

It was getting more and more difficult to see out. As fast as the frost-flowers were cleared from the windscreen they reformed in more opaque patterns, until I could see nothing through them but falling snow; an infinity of snowflakes like ghostly birds, incessantly swooping past from nowhere to nowhere.

The world seemed to have come to an end already. It did not matter. The car had become our world; a small, bright, heated room; our home in the vast, indifferent, freezing universe. To preserve the warmth generated by our bodies we kept close to each other. She no longer seemed tense or suspicious, leaning against my shoulder.

A terrible cold world of ice and death had replaced the

living world we had always known. Outside there was only
the deadly cold, the frozen vacuum of an ice age, life reduced
to mineral crystals; but here, in our lighted room, we were
safe and warm. I looked into her face, it was smiling,
untroubled; I could see no fear, no sadness there now. She
smiled and pressed close, content with me in our home.

I drove at great speed, as if escaping, pretending we could
escape. Although I knew there was no escape from the ice,
from the ever-diminishing remnant of time that encapsuled
us. I made the most of the minutes. The miles and the minutes flew past. The weight of the gun in my pocket was reassuring.

Afterword

One of the worst things about hell is that nobody is ever allowed to sleep there, although it's always night, or at the earliest, about six o'clock in the evening. There are beds, of course, but they're used for other purposes.

—*My Soul in China*

It has been said that Anna Kavan wrote in a mirror. The body of work left by the now obscure British modernist represented a constant inquiry into her own identity, and the invention of a personal mythology—or demonology, as it would become later in her career. The experience of reading Kavan's works one after another, in chronological order, is like hearing the same story repeated again and again, recasting familiar situations and characters in tones that grow more nightmarish as the years pass. Her writing can be seen as an attempt to put into language a lifetime of rejection and alienation. The characters in Anna Kavan's world are travelers of never-ending journeys, by train and by ship; they stop in small, indiscriminate towns where rows of faceless houses are as closed off as their inhabitants, finding strange faces and obstacles everywhere, the landscape one of silent hostility. Her alter egos veer into melancholy and disillusionment and even derangement. They are abandoned orphans seemingly too sensitive for reality.

"So many dreams are crowding upon me now that I can scarcely tell true from false: dreams like light imprisoned in bright mineral caves; hot, heavy dreams; ice-age dreams; dreams like machines in the head." Born Helen Woods in 1901, in Cannes, Kavan was active as a writer from the 1930s through her death in 1968; she wrote about these dreams in some seventeen novels and collections, two published posthumously, which move from first-person essayistic fragments to surrealist experiments, from Freudian fairy tales to metaphysical postapocalyptic fiction. The scope of her writing is breathtaking, although the quality of the output is irregular. Once heralded as the heiress apparent to female experimental writers like Virginia Woolf and Djuna Barnes, and called "Kafka's sister" (and the *K* in her choice of pseudonym, "Kavan," has been read for Kafka, her neighbor alphabetically on the bookshop shelf), she is now only remembered—if at all—for *Asylum Piece*, her exploration of madness, or *Ice*, her sci-fi crossover success.

Despite recurring bouts of mental illness that would result in three suicide attempts, and despite a lifelong addiction to heroin, and in the midst of two failed marriages, Kavan wrote tirelessly and reinvented herself, over and again, in the process eventually taking on the name of one of her earlier heroines. The titles of her novels provide clues as to the transformations of this chameleon, in life as well as in writing: *Let Me Alone* (1930), *A Stranger Still* (1935), *Change the Name* (1941), *Who Are You?* (1963).

Beginning in the late 1920s, Kavan published a string of very good yet conventional novels under the name Helen Ferguson, using the surname of the first husband she abhorred. The Helen Ferguson novels, published by Jonathan Cape with some success, feature young women suffering in suburban miserabilism, trapped by their families and the constraints of gender. There are hints of the sense of persecution and enforced isolation that would inform the later works. *A Charmed Circle*, Kavan/Ferguson's first novel, published in 1929, features two sisters, Olive and Beryl Deane, both unhappy and stuck living in a small manufacturing town—an homage to the schoolteachers Ursula and Gudrun Brangwen in D. H. Lawrence's *Women in Love*. *A Charmed Circle* also calls to mind the delightful weirdness of Jane Bowles's short story "Camp Cataract." The Deane sisters, with their "dark secret faces," live under the tyranny of their hermit father and their dainty mother, who dotes on their cruelly arrogant older brother. "We're all of us miserable, and we all of us hate each other," Beryl complains.

Let Me Alone is based on the author's first year of marriage, which she spent in Burma. Its heroine, named Anna Kavan, is a repressed young orphan who finds herself pushed into marriage by her cruel aunt, forced in the process to give up a scholarship to Oxford. Ferguson portrays the tropics where the new couple settles as an unrelenting, alienating hell. Kavan's husband only wants to control her: "It made him indignant that she still remained somehow apart. It shattered his complacency to think that he had not finally conquered her yet." The character of the sadistic husband was revisited many times by Kavan, and his apotheosis is the narrator in what would be her masterpiece, *Ice*, a man who chases a girl all over the globe so that he can possess her, and the monsoon climax at the end of *Let Me Alone* presages the stylistic power of her later, experimental writing. In the sequel, *A Stranger Still* (1935), the character Anna Kavan is separated from her husband and living in London, where she falls in love with a Sunday painter and heir to a large department store fortune, modeled on Helen Ferguson's somewhat tumultuous love affair with the painter Stuart Edmonds, whom she married in 1928. With Edmonds she traveled through Europe for two years, then settled into a domestic life in Chilterns, Bledlow Cross, where they bred bulldogs—a rural setting utilized for the later Ferguson novels such as *Goose Cross* (1936).

After a suicide attempt in the late 1930s, following the dissolution of her second marriage, Kavan was admitted into a sanatorium, emerging with her new name and persona, as well as with the material for two books that would drastically depart from the tightly controlled realism of the Helen Ferguson years. As has been noted elsewhere, it's almost imperative to speak of Helen Ferguson and Anna Kavan as two different writers. Part of the fascination of the Helen Ferguson years is in the break that occurs along with her assumption of a new identity and style. Like Sylvia Plath's Lady Lazarus, Kavan rose as if from the dead, specter thin because of hospitalization and narcosis. But instead of rising with the red hair of the poem, the former hearty bulldog breeder and brunette girl-next-door bleached hers movie-star blond to mirror the fragile waif, the "glass girl" that would become the nameless heroine in her later works.

First came *Asylum Piece*, her debut as Anna Kavan in 1940, where a desperately unhappy first-person narrator struggles to maintain a dialogue with an increasingly deaf outside world, becoming more and more alienated until she is institutionalized. "I began to feel that if I did not succeed in breaking out of the loathsome circle I should suddenly become mad, scream, perpetuate some shocking act of violence in the open street," she writes. With this collection, Kavan broke from the structure of the conventional novel and began to develop her obsessive dystopian vision. Some of the stories or fragments in *Asylum Piece* can be described as almost diaristic, or essayistic, without much narrative momentum, containing impressions in a style that is sparing and still. These are the dispatches from the inside of a fractured identity. In several of the stories, the first-person narrator undergoes relentless persecution from an anonymous "they" who communicate with her on stiff blue official paper. There is the simple, haunting "The Birthmark," where a schoolgirl happens upon a castle that turns out to be a penal colony for those who do not belong. No one is to be trusted in the world of Kavan's fiction—everybody's a

stranger with a hidden motive. "For how can I tell whether
the person to whom I am talking is not an enemy, or perhaps connected with my accusers or with those who will
ultimately decide my fate?" asks the narrator in "Airing a
Grievance." In a Kavan story, any plotline is subject to distortion, a fog literally or symbolically seeping in. In "The
Birds," the narrator becomes convinced that two brightly
colored birds outside her window in January, "two tiny
meteors of living flame," are in fact hallucinations. Color is
a deception—the world is actually gray and dismal, dissolv-
ing into a dreary fog. In "Machines in the Head," she asks,
"Is it possible that I am still living in a world where the sun
shines and flowers appear in the springtime? I thought I had
been exiled from all that long ago." (According to her biog-
raphy, her wealthy British expatriate parents had sent her
away to a chilly clime in her childhood, and she theorized
that her wet nurse must have hated the cold and transmitted
this aversion in her breast milk.)

At the beginning of World War II, Kavan traveled around
the world, an itinerary complicated by wartime border
restrictions, this atmosphere of paranoia and an unfeeling
bureaucracy further saturating the fiction that came afterward. She passed through New York City several times,
spent six months in California, a setting that would inspire
her posthumously published novella *My Soul in China*,
traveled in Bali, and then spent almost two years in New
Zealand. She returned to London in early 1943, a place she
portrays as simultaneously imprisoning her and driving her
out in the story "Our City," collected in 1945's *I Am Lazarus*. This story and others in the collection document the
communal psychosis caused by the Blitz. Kavan worked as
a researcher in a psychiatric military unit, and in *I Am
Lazarus* she escapes a crushing solipsism at times to tell the
stories of some of its patients.

This is Anna Kavan at her best: exacting, empathetic,
powerful. In the four-page story "Palace of Sleep," an older
doctor gives a young upstart a tour of the narcosis ward. (In

the 1930s and 1940s, Kavan went in and out of various sanitariums and nursing homes for her heroin addiction, where among other treatments she underwent narcosis, a sort of sleeping cure for drug addiction.) In the story, there's the captivating image of a patient in a red dressing gown, shuffling down the corridor with a nurse who calls her Topsy:

> The patient swayed and staggered in spite of the firm grasp that guided her hand to the rail. Her head swung loosely from side to side, her wide open eyes, at once distracted and dull like the eyes of a drunken person, stared out of her pale face, curiously puffy and smooth under dark hair projecting in harsh, disorderly elf-locks. Her feet, clumsy and uncontrolled in their woolen slippers, tripped over the hem of her long nightdress and threw her entire weight on the nurse's supporting arm.

"Welcome to the palace of sleep," the older doctor quips at the story's end. Overall, the pieces in *Lazarus* are less fragmented and claustrophobic, although there are relapses into *Asylum Piece*'s poetic screeds about invisible enemies, as well as a further exploration of the theme of exile, this time in an Antipodean setting. In "The Picture," the narrator is once again living in a foreign country, going to pick up a picture that she had dropped off to be framed the day before. She's excited and optimistic, since the man at the picture shop seemed like a "benevolent gnome." But when she goes back to the shop, she finds herself under surveillance by another man and treated rudely by the dark-haired girl behind the counter who gives her someone else's picture instead. She asks for the old man, hoping for yesterday's touch of humanity, but he pretends not to recognize her: "Then it began to dawn on me that the thing which has so often happened to me in this country had happened again, that I had made a mistake, that I had fallen into the trap of accepting as real an appearance that was merely a sham, a booby trap, a malicious trick."

In the early 1940s Kavan met Dr. Karl Theodor Bluth, who would become her confidante, analyst, and heroin supplier. Kavan and Bluth later authored a dream allegory together, published in 1949 by a specialty press, starring a poetry-spouting circus horse named Kathbar, an amalgam of their two names. Kathbar escapes the slaughterhouse by moving to an artists' colony and founding the existentialist school "Hoofism." Kavan's third known suicide attempt would come in 1964 when Bluth died. Many of the pieces in the posthumously published *Julia and the Bazooka* mourn her longtime analyst, as well as being the only stories to deal directly with her drug use ("bazooka" was the nickname she gave to her syringe).

In the surrealist *Sleep Has His House* (1948), titled *The House of Sleep* in the United States, Kavan attempted to write scenarios directly from her subconscious, incorporating the language and logic of dreams, (calling to mind the prose of Hilda "H. D." Doolittle, another disciple of psychoanalysis, such as *Nights*). The effect of reading *Sleep Has His House* is that of entering a highly coded dream world, and although some of the poetry and imagery is rich, it was shunned both commercially and critically, accused of being pretentious and unreadable.

Still, this collection won Anna Kavan an admirer in Anaïs Nin, who became one of Kavan's staunchest defenders. "Anna Kavan explored the nocturnal worlds of our dreams, fantasies, imagination, and nonreason," Nin writes in her critical study *The Novel of the Future*, which highlighted novelists such as John Hawkes, Djuna Barnes, and Marguerite Young. "Such an exploration takes greater courage and skill in expression. As the events of the world prove the constancy of the nonrational, it becomes absurd to treat such events with rational logic." She also wrote that *Asylum Piece* was "a classic equal to the work of Kafka." Still, as much as Nin admired Kavan, even writing letters to her that remained unanswered, the admiration was not mutual, according to Kavan's biographer David Callard. Kavan was known for dismissing fellow women writers; for instance, she admired the *nouveau roman* but disliked the work of Nathalie Sarraute. However, there were exceptions—she supposedly admired Jean Rhys and Virginia Woolf, as well as Djuna Barnes's *Nightwood*.

In the 1950s, Kavan departed from the subjective first-person experiments of the previous decade to externalize the nocturnal world of the unconscious, the "queer dream plasma which flows along like a sub-life, contemporaneous with but completely independent of the main current of one's existence" (*I Am Lazarus*). The same ideas and images repeat—the chilly, dismal Victorian childhood; the manipulative, glamorous mother; and the two ex-husbands who try to usurp the Kavan-figure's sense of self—but the characterizations become crueler and more fantastical. Although the controlling mother figure is a specter throughout her fiction, Kavan recasts her as a witchy countess modeled on Hans Christian Andersen's Snow Queen in 1956's *A Scarcity of Love*, which Kavan paid some fifty pounds to publish with a vanity press. (Jonathan Cape dropped her after the failure of *Sleep Has His House*; unfortunately, the press that published *Scarcity* went bankrupt soon after the review copies were sent out, and the remaining stock was pulped.) With its Ann Radcliffe mysticism and gothic overtones, *A Scarcity of Love*—a revenge fantasy written right after Kavan's mother died, leaving her with no inheritance—debuts some of the imagery Kavan would use in her adventure stories, as well as the character of the frail girl-child as perfected later in *Who Are You?* and *Ice*.

Eagle's Nest (1957) has been called Kavan's most Kafkaesque work, further developing her concept of a "second secret existence," a real world with an underworld percolating beneath. The nameless narrator in this fantasy is potentially delusional, as in *Ice*, possibly having imagined the fantasy/nightmare world of the "Eagle's Nest," a fortress-like mansion with curious servants and a strange code. The title story of the collection *A Bright Green Field* (1958) moves toward the science fiction of *Ice*, except here it's grass that's the natural force threatening to obliterate humanity—in a "great green grave." The collection also contains the disturbing "Annunciation," about a young girl whose rich, controlling grandmother hides her from the world after her first menstruation, and the beautiful, tragic "Happy Name," in which an old woman returns in a dream to the large Victorian home of her childhood, which she enters through a picture in her nursing home room.

"That's the way I see the world now," Kavan remarked to Peter Owen, her publisher in later years, explaining her gradual shift to science fiction—externalizing the purely mental apocalypses in her earlier works. But *Ice* (1967)—the work that yielded her first mainstream success—transcends genre. To Kavan, the world had ceased to be rooted in reason, and her final and most famous novel articulates her horror of this transformation. A psychosexual adventure story, *Ice* is a fantastical retelling of Kavan's meanderings through the world during World War II. Max Brod once described Kafka's *The Castle* as the "prodigious ballad of the homeless stranger," which could as easily describe *Ice*, inspired by Kavan's travels during the war, and the proximity of New Zealand to Antarctica. In the novel, an anonymous hero must save the world from global destruction—walls of ice closing in amidst war and carnage—all the while chasing the nameless object/victim of desire who haunts him. "She was so thin that, when we danced, I was afraid of holding her tightly. Her prominent bones seemed brittle, the protruding wrist-bones had a particular fascination for me. Her hair was astonishing, silver-white, an albino's sparkling like moonlight, like moonlit venetian glass. I treated her like a glass girl; at times she hardly seemed real." Drugs the narrator takes for his insomnia produce horrific hallucinations in which the girl is thrust into an obstacle course of pornographic violence, resembling Pauline Réage's *Story of O*: she lies bleeding, broken in the white snow, is snatched out of doorways by looming shadows, and is even thrown to a dragon by hostile townsfolk.

The novel was published one year before Kavan died of heart failure, although her death was widely reported as a suicide.

In Kavan's most haunting inquiry into the loss of self, the 1963 novella *Who Are You?*, she rewrote Helen Ferguson's three-hundred-plus page novel *Let Me Alone*. The controlling yet basically harmless husband from that novel becomes the sadistic and alcoholic "Mr. Dog Head," whose activities include raping his wife and bludgeoning rats with his tennis racket. The lonesome yet fiercely independent Anna Kavan is now simply "the girl," yet another blond victim living in a nightmare she can't escape. The title comes from the monotonous song of the birds that live in the tamarind trees in the tropics, whose mechanical and piercing cry mounts in the background throughout the novel. The cries of the "brain-fever birds," which Kavan characterizes as an assault on identity, form an ominous chorus for the main character's breakdown:

> Who-are-you? Who-are-you? Who-are-you? . . . The frantic cries sound to her not only demented but threatening, so that she feels uneasy. Some of them seem to sound distinctly ominous. Yet she must imagine this, for, in reality, all the cries are exactly alike. All have the infuriating, monotonous, unstoppable persistence; all sound equally mechanical, motiveless, not expressing anger, or fear, or love, or any sort of avian feeling—their sole function seems to drive people mad.

This is Kavan's "hot" novel, as opposed to the freeze of *Ice*, with evocative descriptions of heat building once more to a monsoon climax. *Who Are You?* resembles the novels of Robbe-Grillet (the *nouveau roman* was the only school of writing Kavan ever identified with, although much of her work predates it). The novella conjures up an atmosphere of claustrophobia and a stylized and fragmented descent into hysteria, as the young girl begins to lose her identity in the stifling heat. Following an ambiguous first ending, Kavan stages a second, with a different outcome. The result is to destabilize any reality in the preceding narrative, imbuing *Who Are You?* with all the clarity of a fever dream.

The fact that Kavan was able to make art out of a sometimes distorted mirror and so eloquently inquire into the evolution of madness—and let's even call it a feminine madness, although she would have detested the term—is even more extraordinary considering how painful it was at times to live in her version of the world. Kavan portrayed female characters with a desire to fall, to luxuriate at the bottom: shattered women who harbor the hope that someone will come and save them, but who always, in the end, return to the struggles of solitude. These portrayals of women dangling on the brink—or, rather, woman, since it's usually the same character—call to mind Jean Rhys, especially her boozy nihilist Sophia Jansen in *Good Morning, Midnight*, who sets out to drink herself to death and busies herself with the idea of dyeing her hair. Kavan received true recognition for her genius only a year before her death, with the success of *Ice*; interestingly, Rhys's *Wide Sargasso Sea* was published the year before, to much acclaim. Of its success, Rhys famously intoned, "It has come too late." Both Kavan and Rhys were writers many had believed to be dead, Lady Lazaruses who found recognition too late in life to appreciate it. But Rhys is still widely read and accepted as a great modern talent, while Kavan, every bit the equal of every writer she was compared to, has—regretfully—vanished.

KATE ZAMBRENO